EMMA COLE

ECHOES

Remington Carter Series Book One

Emma Cole

Edited by Inked Imagination Services 2020

Edited by Miss Correct All's Editing and Proofreading Services 2019

Cover Art by- Petra J. Knox

Synopsis

When well-laid plans for college went awry, twenty-year-old Remi took it in stride. With events beyond her control taking place and familial responsibility to fulfill, she did the best she could and waited patiently for her turn.

Now, two years later and back on track, albeit a little later than she'd hoped, things are finally looking up. That is until an unforeseen circumstance arises. A flooding in her dorm building has put her into a unique situation that could be just the push she needs to take a chance on the up-and-coming football star that has taken a serious interest in her.

With elements from her past coming back for round two, will Remi be able to juggle it all?

Find out in this first installment of the Remington Carter Series.

NA 18+ due to content.

Prologue

Five years ago…

Under the cloud of disapproval from our father, the driver closes the door on the car as we're sent off for our transgression. It's not the first time we have been uprooted, nor will it be the last.

The only regret we have this time is leaving her.

Whether she has made up her mind on which of us she wanted to be with or not, the other would always be there for her. If it was my brother, I wouldn't begrudge him his happiness just as he wouldn't begrudge me mine. Our father says we're lucky he discovered us, and that, hopefully, 'the girl' as he refers to her, will be too embarrassed to mention it to her own father. Even at sixteen, we know it will be impossible to forget her. I share a look with my brother as we leave the estate.

We'll get her back. Someday, somehow…

Four years ago…

I want to scream and rage.

I know it's not going to do me any good. My father, I could never call him a dad as he isn't that type of parent, would have me shipped back to Australia immediately. The best I can hope for now is to be able to finish school in the States. Even though I recently turned eighteen, I have few options and no resources of my own. It's mid-semester break, and my choices are to return to Brisbane where my mother lives with her new husband, or do as my father commands. As much as I love my mother, I don't want to intrude on her happiness even though she would welcome me with open arms.

No, I have to find a way to get her back, the one I'm being sent away from. According to both of our fathers, who found out what was going on, what we were engaging in was unacceptable behavior. Mostly on my part. As the girl's father put it, I was a 'deviant' who took advantage of his only child. Mine agreed with him, and I was sent back to school four days early. Without a goodbye. I tried to call her, but her number was already disconnected.

One day, I will find her again. They can't keep us apart forever…

Chapter One

In the present…

I stand in line with a housing application along with most of the rest of my coed building. A booth has been set up outside the admissions building to help with foot traffic. A malfunctioning fire sprinkler soaked the first two floors of my building, requiring extensive rehab and displacing about sixty students. Private homes, apartment buildings, and rentals are all offering unused rooms at a discount for the remainder of the semester until the damage can be fixed for anyone that couldn't be placed in other campus housing. Technically, as a sophomore, I could live off-campus already. It had been more convenient as a community college transfer to stay in the dorms for now, so I could get to know my way around.

As I stand in the warm air of early October, I wonder if I'm going to get my application turned in in time to make it to my next class. While I wait, I notice the grass is still green, yet you can smell the crispness in the air signaling Autumn is on its way. Some leaves on the trees have turned colors and begun to fall already.

After another ten minutes of waiting, I finally get to the front of the line to turn my papers in. It's a good thing too since I'm really feeling the need for a bathroom. Maybe I should have held off on the third coffee. The staff member takes my application, pulls off the tabbed number on the bottom, and tells me that the relocations should be settled in the next few hours. She informs me that the rooms have already been secured for the students, and now they just have to be assigned. Any updates will be sent to the students' emails. The school has been right on top of handling the situation. The broken pipes woke everyone up around four this morning, and we are already about to be settled. I get on the main sidewalk and tuck my things into my messenger bag.

As I go to move on to my next and last class of the day, I spot Eli walking towards me. He hasn't seen me yet, and after the day I've had, I would like to keep it that way for now. I quickly hoof it in the other direction towards my class as I think about him. Eli, short for Elliot McAdams. He's the typical "hot" guy on campus. Taller than me, and I'm not short for a woman, blond, and a body like a slim linebacker. He's got muscles upon muscles, but not in a bulky way. Those muscles scream sex on a stick. I've heard more than a few girls comment on how they'd like to touch that body and stare into his dreamy green eyes. Annoying females. He's a sophomore, like me, and plays some sort of catching position on the football team, running back, I think, or something like that. I get all things football mixed up. All the girls are, of course, wild for any popular team player, and being exceedingly attractive only makes it worse. I like him, but I'm not sure if it's worth the drama if it doesn't work out.

I met Eli in my English Lit class. I tripped over a cord on the floor while walking in and fell directly into him. I can and have tripped over my own feet before, so at least I had a legitimate excuse this time. He caught me, and I unintentionally felt exactly how warm and hard that body was. Everywhere. I could see why so many girls were obsessed with touching it. We stood there staring at each other long enough that the professor came in and had to clear his throat to get our attention. I instantly colored up from my neck to my hairline, but Eli just laughed and swept his arm out in a bow to the open seats. We ended up chatting over the next few classes, and he seemed nice. It doesn't hurt to look at him either, which I get caught doing regularly. He's been hinting at a more personal relationship, and I'm undecided as of yet if I want to give him the friend speech or go for it.

As I'm almost to my class, I hear a feminine voice yell my name.

"Remi, wait up!" my best friend since third grade, Alex, yells.

Alexandra Grant is the exuberant half of our duo. With the rockin' curves she's got going on, I'm often amazed at how she keeps it all contained like she does her purple-streaked hair. We met when she moved to my hometown in Connecticut and was the only other girl my age in the sprawling area we lived in. She came up and asked to play, and I shared my hula hoop. We've been mostly inseparable since.

"Hey Alex," I greet her. She's panting slightly after she catches up to me. "What's up?"

Smoothing her purple and blond flyaways, she fixes a stare on me. Totally busted trying to escape. Pretty darn sure Eli knows I'm here now and most likely that I avoided him thanks to the big mouth on the pretty round face of my bff.

"I saw you in line for the housing relocation, but you took off before I could get to you. I also saw a certain football player that seemed to be looking for something. Wouldn't happen to know about that, now would you?" she asks with a brow raised over accusing brown eyes.

I half expect to get another scolding from her on avoiding him. She knows my thoughts on the subject very well, but she can't leave it alone. She'd really like us to get together. Not that I'm opposed, exactly. I just don't have the best luck with guys. Or life in general. I pull myself from my thoughts to answer Alex.

"I was avoiding him." Glancing over her head with my several inch height advantage, I sigh. "We've gone on a few dates. Mostly group things, but the questions are starting to get personal, and he's noticing that I avoid answering a lot of time or change the subject."

Alex gives me a look but doesn't comment for a moment. She knows all the stuff I've had to deal with the last couple of years. She's been a rock during it all for me. I'm the one that had insisted she continue with our plans to go to the university after high school graduation even though I had to take a gap year. My freshman year had been spent at a local community college close to home after my dad disappeared during the summer. Otherwise, I would have been living with Alex instead of in the dorms. We have plans to move in together next semester when Alex's roommate moves out after she graduates and the lease for her expires. Alex's place is a condo right on campus. One of several that her grandparents own and rent out to college students at the university. I had Alex give up my room when I knew I wouldn't be making it to the university for a couple years. Now that her roommate is moving out, I'll be able to move in as soon as the semester is over. She narrows her eyes at me, and I know she's decided to try again.

"I know, Remi, but maybe it's time to let some of that other stuff go, you know?" She looks at me with her hands up. "The stuff with your dad may not ever resolve, and I'm not saying you have to forget, but maybe just try to put it behind you. I know you like him; you get that dopey look on your face when you talk about him. A lot like you used to when you talked about---"

I cut her off before she can go further by putting my hand up.

"Don't, please, Alex. He has never bothered to try to contact me. He knew where I was, and I still never found out where he disappeared to. His dad was very clear he didn't want anything to do with me."

I don't want to talk about that.

Ever.

I finger the necklace at the base of my throat. It was a gift from two wonderful friends that also dropped off the map years ago. I miss them dearly, but I seem to have extremely bad luck with guys. My previous attempts at a love life have turned out disastrous at best.

Also, if I were to ever get my hands on that opportunistic jerk I met later on, he'd better hang onto his balls or I'm liable to remove them. Alex can tell I'm getting worked up when I start harshly twisting long blond strands of hair between my fingers. She pulls the mess from me to untangle it as she quickly jumps in and diffuses the situation.

"Okay, sorry, I won't. It's just that I know you like him even more than you're willing to tell me. We're best friends, so you can't exactly hide it, you know," she says with a smile. "You really should give it a chance, *him* a chance. It'll be different this time. You're an adult and so is he. No one else can make your decisions for you anymore, and I really doubt this one is going to randomly take off since he is enrolled in school and football here."

"I'll admit it. I like him, a lot actually. That's partially why I've been avoiding him. Also, I'd have to talk to him about everything if we got serious. At least some of it. I'm just not sure I want to do that yet. So, now I have to get to class or I'm going to be late. See you later?" I turn to walk off.

"I need to get to class myself or I'd stay and badger you longer. Let me know when you're ready for help with moving your things today." Alex smirks. "Unless you want to get Eli to help you out instead. I'm sure he'd be happy to just be around you." Nothing like your best friend playing matchmaker; you can tell them to shut it, and they completely ignore you.

"I know he'd help in a minute." I snort. "Not sure I want to face him so soon after getting caught ignoring him though."

I wave as I part ways with Alex, letting her know I'll text her if I need help with my things. I haven't really unpacked my belongings since I was only going to be in the dorms for the first semester until I moved in with Alex. I shouldn't need any help as it's mostly clothes and some little things like toiletries that won't be much trouble to move around.

I make my way to my classroom and sit through it without really hearing most of what the professor says. On the bright side, it's a course that almost directly follows the reading, so I should be able to catch up easily from my textbook.

On my way out of the class, I pull out my phone as it buzzes with a notification. Checking the screen, I see I have an email from the campus housing authority already. I open it, and it's the contact info for Samantha Barrett, Administrative Assistant for Grayside Security. Confused as to why I would be staying at a business, I look it up on the internet, finding that the company occupies only two of the levels in the building. From the picture of the building, I'm assuming there are apartments on the other floors. Security firm with housing? Count me in. I call the number listed as I walk out onto the quad.

Elliot

She walked away.

I know she saw me, and she just pretended not to and walked away. I want to rub my chest where it hurts from the disappointment. I know I shouldn't have such strong feelings for her yet, but it is what it is. They're there, and they're not going to go away anytime soon. I need to find a way to get her to talk to me without scaring her off. Something is bothering her about being more than friends, and I really don't think she feels comfortable enough with me yet to tell me what it is.

I sigh and start to make my way to practice. I have to greet the new roommate that Ethan agreed to take in for the university when I get home, then I'll try to see if I can get Remi to hang out with me tonight.

Chapter Two

Remington

The building I walk up to isn't far from the Everston campus. It's a brownstone that has a discreet placard out front with Grayside Security and a key logo on it. From appearances, the lower floors are for the business and the living quarters are on an upper level. I follow Samantha, the administrative assistant, who was waiting out front to meet me.

She's in a ridiculously snug pencil skirt and jacket combo that displays her considerable assets. We come up to a side entrance that she unlocks with a key. Walking into a foyer area, there is another door with a keypad, and she punches a code. Waiting until the light turns green, she opens the door.

When I step in, I see it leads to a landing for a stairway going both up and down. The foyer had been done with a tastefully minimalist style in tones of gray and white with industrial carpeting and textured walls with three doors, and the trend continues into the stairwell.

Gesturing with lacquered nails and a toss of curly auburn hair, Samantha indicates a closed door. "There is an elevator, but it's the older cage type, and it's faster to use the stairs unless you have a lot to carry. The owner wanted to keep as much of the original hardware in the building as possible as long as it still had functionality." Her bright blue eyes convey her distaste as does her scrunched up pert little nose.

She seems to not appreciate the idea of the old-fashioned elevator while I can't wait to see and ride in it. I'll wait until later and explore on my own as I don't believe that would go over well at the moment.

"That's alright. I don't mind taking the stairs." I try to be diplomatic.

I follow Samantha up to the third floor; she informs me the fourth floor is a private area and the first two floors are for the business. When I ask exactly what the business is and who runs it, she just vaguely says it's a security firm and that the owner is very private in a manner that implies it is none of my business. Odd, with them being a company. I decide I'll look it up later after I get settled. Samantha gives off the vibe she'd rather be doing anything other than this.

She opens the door on the third floor and goes inside. I follow her in then just stop and stare. The whole place is an open floor plan with exposed beams and hardwood floors with rugs scattered here and there.

The rugs vary in color depending on the area they are in. The ones in the kitchen are all jewel-toned blue and purple, while the dining area is scattered with thin metallic pewter and black rugs. Further in, there's a hallway lined with doors that ties the living/kitchen area together with an almost forest green runner accented by gold and copper. The kitchen is all brushed stainless-steel appliances and ebony marble countertops along with a matching breakfast bar. A huge off-white leather sectional couch takes center stage in the common area with overstuffed pillows large enough to double as chairs around the coffee table. Weirdly enough, it all comes together nicely. The walls are alternating basic tones that also flow well together.

The biggest flat screen I've ever seen takes up most of a wall with a recessed media center and all sorts of consoles underneath it. Someone must be a gamer around here. Potted leafy plants in stone urns help break the areas up a little. Off to the other side of the kitchen/living area is a large, mahogany, rectangle dining table that looks to seat eight. Beyond that an alcove type area, if you can call it that since it's actually pretty big, has bookshelves lining the walls and easy chairs with lamps on tables next to them. This place is absolutely amazing, and I can't believe I'll be staying here.

"Are the owners around? I'd like to meet them and thank them for allowing me to stay until repairs are made to the dorm."

I am also really curious about who else I will be living with.

"Most of the guys are out of town right now, but one of the roommates will be here later on today. I'll give you your codes and keys and show you your room. All the other rooms are locked with codes as well, so you won't have access to them. I'm not sure if they'll wrap up their current job and get back while you're here or not. They stay very busy, so you probably wouldn't see them much even if they were here. Normally, they wouldn't have a female stay with all males. I guess someone at the housing authority thought you were a boy. With a name like Remington I can't say I blame them for the mix up." She says it flippantly with an airy hand wave, like I haven't heard similar things about my name all my life. I don't particularly care and ignore her cattiness as she continues on.

"I tried to tell them that the owner only wanted another guy here, but they said all the other spaces have been allotted and they've already paid for it. If you don't stay here, you'll have to find alternate lodging on your own and wait until the owners are back to get a refund for reimbursement. Being that there really isn't anywhere else left, they're stuck with you until they return. Unless you have somewhere else you would like to stay? If so, I can let the owner and the university know."

She's acting weirdly happy about the prospect. Unfortunately for her, I don't have an alternative.

In my head, I'm flipping her off. I would love to tell her I won't be staying and that obviously it's not her decision to make regardless of her thoughts on the subject. Instead, I keep my mouth closed and decide to accept the room. Alex can't have anyone for more than three days at a time, a rule that was enforced the last time her roommate's boyfriend overstayed his welcome. I don't want to have to ask her to do that unless it's a last resort.

I *do* have money, and I could get a motel for a few days, but the ones close to campus are already full. I'd have to drive a bit, and with my schedule it would be back and forth a lot unless

I stayed in the library to study. I'll stick around for now. I can always take off to Alex's if I need to.

Next to Samantha in her skirt and jacket combo with heels, I'm feeling a little shabby in flats, jeans, and a t-shirt, all I have at the moment since very little of my clothing escaped getting wet. I tower over Samantha, not winning the petite award for sure. Although I'm not heavy, so I have that going for me.

Actually, I'm very skinny, mostly from running, and I get to eat all the time due it as well. Usually I'm not insecure, but this woman has me feeling close to it. Add to that my slightly larger than average chest and it's perfect for the modeling I do on the side to supplement my student aid. I get the catty reaction from lots of other girls and women about it. As soon as they find out I model, it's like they have a switch for insta-witch. Modeling isn't the easiest thing ever, but few people seem to know that. Most of the time it's fun, but imagine having to just stand in the cold or the heat for hours without showing that the temperature is affecting you or it will ruin the pictures. Ever stood in the snow in heels and lingerie? I don't recommend it. I didn't want to spend years paying huge loans if I could help it. It helps a lot that I'm able to make good money for part-time work, so I'm not complaining about it.

"I'm sure it will be fine or work itself out," I finally say. I'm not going to be put off by someone acting territorial over people I've never even met. "Do you know what time the roommate will be here? I want to go grab what I can tonight, but I don't want to be in his way."

Taking charge of the conversation, I steer it in the direction I need to get this wrapped up. I have things to do, and I would like to get to them sooner rather than later. Chick has gotta go.

Samantha replies, "He should be back after practice around six or so. If he needs me for anything regarding the arrangement, you have my number and can have him give me a call."

She turns and goes down the hall, gesturing I should follow. Opening a door, she indicates this is my room and shows me the en suite bathroom that also connects with the room that's through the other door. "This locks from both directions. One of the guy's bedrooms is on the other side, and it will stay locked until they're back."

It makes sense now why they would want another man to room here. I did think it slightly odd that a guest room would have a shared bathroom like this, but maybe it was from before it was converted.

After Samantha says goodbye and takes her leave, I poke around a little, checking things out. The fridge is partially stocked with a mix of healthy and junk food; the pantry is much the same. When I say pantry, I really mean store aisle. That thing is as big as a walk-in closet, and in the back of it there is a large chest freezer. I decide to make a quick run back to the dorm to pack up what I can this afternoon. After I see there is a separate laundry room, I get excited at not having to go off-site to wash everything that got wet. Yay to not lugging laundry around. With a little luck, I can have my clothes clean by tonight and my other things out of the dorm and unpacked into my new room before dinner. Thankfully, most of my belongings are still packed away in a small storage unit where they'd been in anticipation of moving in with Alex. It shouldn't take me long with the things I *do* have.

❧ ❧ ❧

I head to my dorm and make it through the crowd of other residents trying to move their things. It takes three trips to get everything down to my car, and I read the instructions one more time to make sure I didn't forget anything. The housing authority wants each room to be left the same way. Apparently, the flood restoration company told them they could work faster and get the clean up done sooner if everything was already moved to specific spots in the rooms to make them all uniform. I find my roommate Cindy filling a box as I go back into the room. She's come back for a few odds and ends, and I help her with arranging the room as requested.

"Hey, I was wondering when you were coming. I saw the notice that they want everyone out by seven tomorrow morning." Cindy is nice, but I don't really know her that well. Being a sophomore in a freshman dorm makes things interesting. She mostly hangs out with a different crowd than I do.

"Yeah, I was meeting my contact for the apartment I'm staying in. At first I thought it was a mistake. I got assigned the Grayside Security building right off campus."

Cindy squeals and jumps up and down. I'm a little stunned at the reaction; this is the most emotion she's shown towards me since she found out I was only with her for a semester. She had wanted a *proper roommate* to experience college with. Her words. I'm not sure why we wouldn't have been able to be friends regardless, but she *is* a tad weird.

"O.M.Geee I am so jealous." Really? Why do girls act like that? She even jumps up and down and claps her hands together. Hands that have cotton candy pink nails. I wear what I have to for work, but Cindy is a girly girl that's always done up like a pre-stepford wife. "Those guys are so hot, and they never let girls over there from what I hear. Rumor is there was a fiasco with one awhile back. She worked for a rival company and tried to steal files or something like that. Let me know if you want to trade places because I will so gladly switch with you." Cindy finally takes a breath and stops talking after I shake my head no.

I'm not sure how much of a hassle that would be, and after I see how others would jump at the chance, I sort of understand some of Samantha's attitude. I would feel bad subjecting strangers to Cindy and whatever friends she might take over with her. Now I'm more curious than ever about who I will be living with.

Chapter Three

I park my canary yellow 67′ Mercury Cougar next to the side door so I can unload. It's not quite in pristine condition. One of the things my dad helped me do since I got too old for "Dad" activities was to restore my "Bird." He nicknamed my car that for the color and thought it was hilarious that the model was a cat.

My dad has an odd sense of humor.

Or had.

Not really sure at this point. Really, it was the only thing we'd ever bonded over after about the age of six or seven when my tastes got too girly for him. Shaking off the memories, I pop the trunk to get started.

❦ ❦ ❦

After getting everything lugged upstairs I remember there's an elevator and figure I'll have to try it out another time. I get a load of laundry started before beginning to unpack. The sooner I finish, the more time there will be to check everything out.

The bathroom is all browns and creams with a lot of mirrors and good lighting. It actually has a deep jacuzzi tub, and I think I'm in love with whoever put this in here. It also has a separate stall shower done in dark brown tile. My room is off-white with beige carpet and the rest of the room is maroon and mauve. I imagine the owner must have had some help from a decorator with all of this color. It's all really nice for a bunch of guys. Heck, even girls I know don't decorate or coordinate this well.

After getting what I can put away, I decide to run to the local supermarket. I don't want to impose and eat the food that's already in the kitchen, feeling that would be a little rude and a bad way to start off being here. I'm sweaty from packing things back and forth but want to get dinner started before I shower. Sniffing myself I shrug and decide to brave the store without one.

I quickly grab enough groceries for a few days, hoping the other resident won't mind me cooking. Maybe he'll be more likely to let me stay if I cook for him. After what Samantha said, I'm nervous. I just need to get through this semester, and I'll be back on track.

Usually, college guys live on ramen and Easy Mac unless they go out to eat. So, I decide to make extra as it couldn't hurt my case.

I make it back to the apartment and get everything put away. After, I throw together a vegetable salad and a meatloaf and clean up after myself.

Before I forget, I switch my laundry over and start another load with my favorite laundry soap. It has a complementing fabric softener and dryer sheets, so I rarely even worry about perfume. It smells like sunshine. At least, that's what the person who gave me my first bottle said it smelled like and that it reminded him of me. It's a little hard to find as it was a brand that was mostly carried in the UK, but now it's migrated this way.

After I unpack my toiletries and some of my clothes, I decide to take a quick shower. I have enough time, as I see it's a few minutes until six, and the food still has a while to cook.

As I'm stepping out of the shower, I hear some noise, and then a familiar voice yells, "Hey, something smells good in here. Since you're inside, I'm assuming Samantha must have shown you around."

Footsteps come closer, muffled by the rugs but still audible. He's not actually going to come in here, is he? Oh, crap he probably thinks I'm a guy! Before I can announce myself or even get to the door to lock it, I hear a quick tap tap, and the handle turns right as I get my towel almost fastened. A head pokes in with, "I just wanted to let you know the towels are in the hall closet. It's all toiletries and cleaning supplies under the cupboard in here..." He trails off as he sees me.

Suddenly, his eyes go wide when he realizes it's me, and they travel the length of my towel-wrapped body. "Remi? What are you doing in here?" I see him trying to look around me for someone else.

I'm tomato red and trying to make sure I'm fully covered. Of course, it would have to be Eli living here with the way my luck has been going today. Cindy did say hot guys live here. I have to agree with her. Wait, that means she likes *my* hot guy. Nope, not happening.

"Um. Well, this is where I was assigned to stay. I hope it's not a problem." When he doesn't answer, I gesture to my towel-clad self. "Can I get dressed? I'll be right out." At that he snaps out of his trance and has the grace to look embarrassed that he barged in on me.

"Of course, sorry, here's the towel" He leaves the towel on the counter and backs out shutting the door.

Once dressed, I take the time to compose myself. I put on some moisturizer and comb my hair before grabbing a hairband on my way out. It'll just have to air dry for now.

Going out into the main area, I find Eli inspecting the contents of the oven. He looks up and comments, "This looks great. I wasn't planning on my new roommate feeding me." He smiles sheepishly. "Sorry this is awkward; I wouldn't have walked in if I'd known there was a girl in there. I know the guys requested that another man stay when they were asked about putting someone up. Not that they don't like women, but with four guys living here it made more sense."

He's rambling and knows it. I try to hide my grin. It's kinda cute to see him out of sorts. I notice him eyeing my fuzzy yellow socks. My feet are always cold, and I have many pairs of fuzzy socks.

"Those are cute." My grin gets bigger, and his eyes round out to match. "I said that out loud, didn't I?" I nod, deciding to rescue him.

"Samantha, the lady that brought me here, did mention something about that. She figured it was my name that threw them off and they must not have paid attention. She said it shouldn't matter anyway as the other guys are gone. I didn't get the names of the occupants, so I didn't know you lived here. Is it gonna be okay that I stay? At least for tonight? I can go stay with Alex for a few days and figure something else out if not. I don't want to make you uncomfortable."

"No, it will be alright. You're pretty normal for a girl, and I'll vouch with the guys," he jokes. "They should have the dorms fixed pretty soon, I think. Samantha is the administrative assistant for the company. I'm surprised she was so cordial. She's not always so nice to other women."

He's quiet for a minute, looking like he wants to say something, but not sure how to. "So, you've been avoiding me."

Since that didn't sound like a question, more a statement, I'm thinking I'm busted. That means he knows I saw him earlier and ignored him. Well, that's awkward. I wince a little and look at him, noticing he's still flushed from practice. He must have showered in the locker room as his blond hair is still wet and combed back. He is pretty hot. How am I going to cope with being around him so much? I've avoided any seriousness, not because I'm not interested, but I wanted to have the normal college experience for a while without the drama of attachments. To be on my own and experience things for myself.

I hoped he would understand. I decide just to be honest and tell him all that.

"Eli, I'm not leading you on. I have had some things to deal with in my personal life, and I wanted not to have any complications for now. I don't mean you're a complication, just that a new relationship generally is, and I haven't even made many new friends yet. Is that alright?"

He nods once and puts his hands in his pockets like it's to avoid reaching out and touching me. I continue on, changing the subject, "I also bought some groceries. I didn't want to get into what was already in here. I wasn't sure what you guys liked, so if you want something else for dinner, I won't be offended." He seems to be taking this rather well.

"Oh, no, it smells great in here. I can cook basics, but I will enjoy the cooking while I can. Maybe you can teach me some things while you're here. My mom tried but said it was a lost cause. That was also before I had to eat my own cooking. Now I have a better appreciation for those lessons. Do you need any help with anything?"

"You can set the table if you don't mind. I'll start pulling everything out. I'd be happy to show you what I know. For now, you can set the table if you don't mind. The meatloaf should be done by now."

I walk around him and go to the oven, trying not to be obvious as I check out his well-worn t-shirt and low hanging jeans. I look down at his adorable, bare feet. That vee guys' hips make is extra pronounced, and I want to reach out and touch it. Instead, I turn to pull the meatloaf out of the oven, slice it, and put it on a serving dish before I get caught ogling him. I take the covered salad out of the fridge along with some dressing, Greek Goddess. A friend recommended this on her social media page, and it looked good, so I tried it. I haven't eaten anything else since.

"I hope you like the dressing. It's one of my favorites, but Alex says it's gross." I wrinkle my nose in protest. I take everything over to the table that Eli has set and go to sit down, but he beats me to it, pulling out my chair and sliding it in as I sit. At least I didn't mess it up; I always feel awkward when someone else helps me in my seat.

"I'm sure it will be fine. I like just about anything. So," he continues after we dish up, "did you get everything you need from your dorm room? If not, we can run over there after dinner."

"I got everything I need, thank you though. Everything I didn't immediately need was put in storage until I move in with Alex next semester. That's when the lease for her roommate is up. The rest fit in my car."

Eli grows quiet over the course of dinner. By the time we're almost finished eating, the silence has become uncomfortable, and now he has a determined look on his face. Ah, shit, I knew it. He's gonna bring it up. I tense, waiting for what he's going to say.

"If you weren't interested in anything except friendship, you could have just told me. I wouldn't have held it against you. 'Dealing with stuff?' I'm not stupid, Remi. What else would you say when you need to stay here and I could fuck it up for you?" He glares at me with a wounded look on his face. "I wouldn't do that, even if you don't want to be with me. I don't have a problem with you being here."

"Eli, it's not that I wasn't interested, but if you want to be an ass about it, maybe for now it's probably best to be friends. Especially with the fact that we're going to be living together for the near future."

I don't know what else to say without making the situation worse. I never thought it was really that big a deal. "To be perfectly clear, I thought you, the jock, wanted a fling with the model. I do hear your friends. I'm not stupid either, Eli, and I've not heard you say anything differently. You seemed genuinely nice, but I really have things going on, and right now they're not your business. If you don't want me here, just say so, and I'll leave."

I'm so pissed that I want to yell some more. Thankfully, I count to ten in my head instead, and it helps. Fighting with Eli the first day I'm here isn't what I wanted.

Eli stays quiet for a moment, then gets up, thanks me for dinner, and wishes me goodnight after clearing his dishes. He walks down the hall without turning back and disappears into his room.

Now that I'm getting over my mad, I start to feel bad that I probably hurt his feelings. It's not what I intended. I put the leftovers away and make my own way to bed. I have a long day of classes ahead tomorrow.

Chapter Four

As I'm lying in bed, I think about the times I've been out with Eli. The first time was after a game. Alex and her roommate Gina were waiting on Gina's boyfriend to get out of the locker room.

Since Alex and I were planning on doing something together, I was with them. That's when Eli came out of the locker room with Gina's boyfriend. I just stared at him. He was extremely good looking, and he came out with a confident swagger like a lot of attractive guys do. When he caught me staring, I blushed, but he only stared back, smiling. After he made some idiotic comment about it being his birthday and strippers, I turned and started walking away while Alex busted out laughing so hard she was bent over to catch her breath. He took off after me, apologizing and saying how he thought I would find it funny.

Well, obviously I hadn't found it funny. I stood there glaring at him while he asked if I would go bowling with him and some other team members to make it up to me. Alex and I went and actually had a good time. He did cute things like 'helping me with my form' or pulling me into his lap. He was so sweet about it that I didn't find it creepy or uncomfortable. We had an immediate connection, and I made a conscious effort to enjoy myself.

That was the start of weekly group things I'd gone on with Eli since school started, each one bringing us closer. Now I was wondering in all that time, why he hadn't ever invited me over. I had never really thought about it before. Must be that rule that him and Samantha had talked about. Come to think of it, my roommate Cindy said something too. I'd have to ask later.

We'd also had one sort of date at a frat party. I had gotten ridiculously drunk, and Eli ended up carrying me back to my dorm where I tried to make out with and probably go further with him. He nicely told me that he wasn't having sex with me drunk, took off our shoes and jeans, and cuddled with me until I fell asleep. I woke up alone the next morning, extremely relieved that he was a good guy and mortified at what I remembered.

Now we were living together, sort of, however temporary it was going to be. I *needed* to make this better. I wasn't going to get to sleep until I did.

I throw the covers back and head for Eli's room. I don't see a light under the door, but I'm almost positive he didn't leave. I knock on the door before I lose my courage. For a minute, I don't think he's going to answer, and I've turned around to leave when I hear a "Come in."

I open the door and find Eli in some plaid flannel pajama pants. All I can do is stare. Uncovered, that vee is something else. His abs are washboard, his waist very trim. His chest is just as muscled and huge as his biceps. He turns to sit on his bed, and I gulp when I see his back. It's as defined as the rest. I want to run my hands all over his body and never stop. Then repeat the action with my tongue. My panties get damp at the thought and I hope it's not noticeable with the thin pajama pants I have on. My nipples are already at attention under the cami I'm wearing.

As I step into his room, I'm all of a sudden very nervous. Licking my lips draws the attention of his eyes, and they heat at the small action. I can't deny the mutual attraction we have, so I screw my courage up.

"Can we talk?" I stand there with my arms wrapped around my torso, waiting on him to answer.

"Sure, why not?" That's not the best answer, yet it's probably better than I should expect. I make my way to his desk chair and pull it closer in front of where he's sitting on the edge of his bed.

"Okay, so I'm not sure what to say. I saw this going differently in my head." I chuckle a little in a self-deprecating way. I blow out a breath and look up to make eye contact. "I'm not very good at this. The relationship thing. I've been avoiding it. I haven't said no because, well, I really don't *want* to say no. I like you a lot, Eli. Probably more than I should this soon." I tuck my legs up under me and wait to see if he'll say anything. I'm really not good at talking about these things.

"Why didn't you just say that in the first place? I think I would have understood or at least tried to. I have feelings for you, Remi, serious ones. I don't get serious about girls; I like to have a good time. I'm not going to say I'm innocent. I'm not. Usually if I hit on you and don't get anywhere the first few tries, that's it, I move on. There's something different about you though. I want to know what you think, what you like. The good and bad. I've never wanted something like that before. That might make me sound shallow, but it's the truth." He runs his fingers through his hair, making the muscles in his stomach flex. I can't stop staring. I know he's watching, but even with that I can't seem to make myself stop. He starts laughing. "If I would have known that was going to be your reaction, I would have taken my shirt off a long time ago."

I look up at him again. Completely ignoring his comment, I say, "So you're not mad at me anymore?" I pull my bottom lip from my teeth again.

"No, I'm not mad. Come here, Remi girl."

Reaching out, he pulls me up and between his legs. Firmly, he wraps his arms around my hips and buries his face in my stomach, making me gasp. I feel his grip tighten, then slowly his fingertips run under the edge of my shirt, making tingles race all over my body. He leans back and pulls me with him so I'm lying on top of him.

With the hardness pressing into my belly, I can tell that he's feeling about the same as I am. So I wiggle against him a little, drawing a groan out of him before leaning down, so my chest brushes his. I bring my face down closer until our breath mingles, and he doesn't move, waiting on me to make up my mind. I lightly brush my lips across his and sigh. That's all the incentive he needs to flip us over and cage me in. He takes my mouth in a rough kiss, holding himself above me in a pushup position, while I tangle my hands in his hair, finding it's soft and thicker than mine. The little bit of stubble on his jaw that's grown since he shaved this morning scrapes against my face, heightening the sensations. Every touch makes my breath come a little shallower, and a moan escapes when his hand brushes up against the outer edge of my breast. The sound seems to bring Eli back some, and he pulls up with a pained expression on his face.

"Not that I don't want to keep doing this, but I think we should stop here. I want to do more, so much more." He rests his forehead on mine then gets up and pulls me with him. Taking my hand, he walks me back to my room. He pulls me close, kisses the top of my head, and shoos me into my room. I'm a little confused at the abruptness but also a little thankful. He didn't have to stop, and he knows it, but he did anyway. I climb back into bed and fall asleep remembering his arms around me.

Eli

I have to say, I didn't see that coming. Trying to talk to Remi had gone all sorts of wrong. First, I was surprised by her being here.

And trying to get the picture of her wet and in a towel out of my head was going to take a long while. I was already so frustrated about her avoiding me earlier, and then she had planned to continue to ignore it until I brought it up.

I want her. Badly.

Apparently, she wants me just as much, but something is holding her back. Which is why I stopped where we did, but it definitely left me with a massive case of blue balls. I contemplate taking care of it, but the need for sleep wins out.

My last thought is if chasing her isn't working out, I'm going to make her come to me. It had worked out tonight.

Chapter Five

The next few days fall into a pattern. I go to class and see Eli in the class we share. Later in the evening, at home with the dinners I make. He starts helping with meals and is an excellent student. Soon he'll be able to cook a full menu by himself. He makes small talk if I initiate it, but nothing further. No invitations to hang out with friends or privately. I'm not sure what to make of it. I think this may be his way of backing off and letting me process.

I talk to Alex some, and she asks what's going on as I haven't really talked about it much. I fill her in on what's happened, and her suggestion is to make a move on him. I promise to take her idea under consideration.

The rest of the week is much the same except the shoot I have Wednesday afternoon. I don't have classes other than art history early in the morning.

I get to my shoot for a clothing magazine thirty minutes early with a bag containing a brush, hair ties, lotion, makeup, and adhesive remover. You never know what you're going to get put in, and tape leaves a sticky residue on your skin. After placing my bag in one of the cubbies, I head over to the shoot manager and photographer. At the same time, a woman comes from the wardrobe area. She introduces herself and the two men before I get sent to the wardrobe changing area for my first outfit.

They get everything set up, and the photographer starts taking photos. I lose my concentration a bit when I feel as if I'm being watched.

Looking around, I try to pick out what's giving me the feeling but don't see anyone doing anything strange. Nor even really paying more attention than they should. The shoot is off campus in the next city over, a suburb of New York City.

It reminds me that my mom hates that I'm so far away, but it's where Alex and I wanted to go. With the campus being located rurally, it's enough to avoid the big city crush. We continue on, and I shrug off my feeling of being watched.

When I get home, I find I have a voicemail. Alex asking me to go to a sorority party on Friday night. I mention it to Eli, but he says he's gonna hang with some of the guys at one of their places instead and for me to have fun.

Once again, he blows me off when usually he would be the one asking me to hang out. Something is up with him and it's starting to bug me.

Friday night finds me at Alex's place in her very messy bedroom. I mean, it looks like her closet had a gremlin in it that ate after midnight. Clothes are scattered and draped over every available surface. Alex is a little shorter than me but as curvy as I am. She has me try on outfit after outfit, finally settling on a slinky silver wrap dress.

On her, it would be a decent length. On me, it's entering mini territory. If I'm not careful, my lacy boy shorts are going to make an appearance. Alex hands me a pair of silver stilettos that match the dress. Thankfully, I have small feet for my height, and we're the same size. I'm sure I'm going to be the tallest girl there at this point, although I do have to admit they make my legs look killer.

"Remi," Alex says, fighting me for the material we both refuse to let go of, "take the bra off. You can't just tuck the straps in! You can see them. It will be fine, I promise. A lot of girls will be dressed in much less. All the important parts are covered, more's the shame. Now, how do I look?"

Alex turns a full circle in a bright pink spaghetti strap dress that hits mid-thigh. She's paired it with matching, chunky-heeled shoes. You'd think I would be okay with showing skin, but working and playing are two very different things. At work, I don't have to worry that I will flash a room full of people my goods. If people that I have to see and go to class with see me in a magazine, they don't always make the connection. It's not like my bio is printed with the catalog.

"You look beautiful, as usual." Alex has her hair up with pieces hanging down here and there. She looks like a fifties sex pot, and it works for her. She's always a magnet for guys *and* girls, a social butterfly if there ever was one. If it wasn't for her, I would probably stay in my room with my fuzzy socks and a book.

I sigh, knowing I'm not getting out of this. I kinda just want to go find Eli, but it's friend duty time. I'll corner Eli after I get home and make him fess up.

"Alright." Alex starts ticking off points on her fingers. "Hair: check, hot and sexy makeup: check, drool-worthy dresses: double check. Let's go." We grab our jackets and head out for the party. I instantly feel the chill on my legs. Fall is definitely here. Our heels click on the pavement as we make our way the couple blocks to the house. I'm glad it's not far as these are in no way to be considered walking shoes. I'm wondering how long until I can put the flats on that I snuck into my bag without Alex noticing.

Eli

I wanted to go to the party with Remi. I actually had been going to turn my friend's video game marathon down and go before I found out she had already made plans to attend with Alex. I don't want to be the proverbial third wheel. A few other guys from the team were going and had invited me. In keeping with the plan of making her come to me when she's ready instead of continuously chasing her, I text my friend back that I'm coming over and let the guys know that I'm going to stay in tonight.

Remi

As we near the sorority house, I hear the music from a block away. When we finally get inside, we're instantly bombarded with friendly bodies. One of the house girls that we both know drags us to the kitchen to get drinks. Amanda, I think her name is.

"Keep an eye on your drinks. Most everyone here is fine, but you always get those few dicks that feel the need to be assholes." She points at us, waving her finger between the two of us.

Okaayy. Nice to know. I don't think any of us are under illusions of what happens with said dicks.

Alex and I make our way further into the house and out to the patio. It's pretty chilly out there, so we don't stay long. Inside, Alex sees a guy she's been talking to that she likes and asks if I want to come with. I wave her off telling her I'm fine; I'm just gonna watch the dancers.

The place is packed and getting hot from all the bodies. Pretty soon an arm slides around my waist. I hear an unfamiliar voice say, "Hey baby, I've seen you standing around. Want to come hang with me instead?"

Lamest pickup line ever. Get lost, dude.

"No thank you," I reply, trying to be polite for now. Obviously, the guy is a little trashed. But he isn't taking no for an answer.

He's actually attractive when I turn and look, but his attitude is all ugly. A hand cuts in between us. "Well, there you are. I've been looking for you." A guy steps between me and the grabber, and the grabber doesn't look very appreciative.

"Remi, how about that dance you promised me?" I have no idea who this guy is although he does look a little familiar. Light brown hair, browns eyes, and a strong square jaw. He's actually pretty good looking as well, trim and fit, in a light blue button-up that's open with a fitted light gray t-shirt underneath.

"Oh, there you are. I was just looking for you too!" I turn to extract myself from the other guy that has ahold of me with a gleeful expression.

Sayonara, asshat!

He looks confused as he looks from me to the interloper and back again. I don't think he can decide if we're lying or not. He begrudgingly lets go and stalks off into the party.

Good riddance.

"Hey, thanks for that. I was trying to think of a non-witchy way to extract myself. No offense, but how do you know my name?" May as well get straight to the point, don't need grabby hands two point oh.

"We have Eastern Studies together. I usually sit a couple rows behind you. My name's Adam." He smiles at me, and it lights his whole face up. His name isn't really ringing any bells though. I'm mostly sure he's not lying, so I try to figure it out.

And then feel bad I didn't ever really notice him. Although that would explain why he seemed familiar. I go for honesty. I really can't place him, so faking it won't work, and he did come to my rescue after all.

"Sorry, I don't really know too many people here yet. I only transferred in this semester." Yep, play the 'I'm new card'.

"That's okay, I've seen you around some. I've been meaning to introduce myself, but you usually disappear pretty quickly after class, and I either see you with your friend you came in with tonight or Elliot and his gang. I'm glad I finally got the chance to talk to you. Since you said that you promised me one, do you want to dance?"

"If I recall correctly, *you* said I promised, and I just agreed with you. I think I can handle that though, but no squashing my toes." With that, we move over into the cleared area being used as a dance floor. A slow song comes on, and surprisingly, Adam moves pretty well. I wrack my brain, trying to find something to talk about. "The girl is my best friend Alex. We've been mostly inseparable since third grade. Do you come to a lot of these parties?"

"A few here and there. I'm glad I came tonight though. Elliot's not with you?" He looks around like Eli is going to pop up. This close I can see copper flecks in his brown eye; it makes them almost too pretty for a man. He seems like a happy person. I think I like him already.

"He decided to skip it and go to a friend's house instead. I promised Alex we would go out, so here I am. How do you know Eli?"

"I'm part of the training crew for the football team. I'm one of the medical techs since I'm specializing in sports medicine here. I see a lot of the players to make sure they're wrapped properly, check out strains, help with their exercise routines, ect." I can tell he's downplaying it some. I wonder if he's embarrassed that he's not a player. He doesn't seem the type to care too much about that though.

"So, you take care of the players if they get hurt and do things to prevent them from getting hurt?"

"Yes, that about sums it up. I've heard Elliot talk about you a few times and again today at practice. When I put together that you were the same girl I've been trying to get the courage up to talk to, I figured I had better use the next opportunity to do so before I lost my chance.

And here you are." Huh, well then. Not sure what to say here.

I repeat the last part of that thought, out loud this time. I see his face fall a little.

"Should I take that comment as I'm too late or that you're not interested?" he asks carefully. I can tell he's trying to hide his disappointment. I have to give him points for that. He's not being like some other guys when you tell them no. He's actually being pretty decent.

"I wouldn't say not interested. Romantically, probably not. Friends? I'm most definitely open to. Would that be alright with you?"

I'm not sure what else to say. He's nice and attractive, but I feel vaguely guilty like I'm sneaking around on Eli. I know there's not really any reason for that, but I still feel it just the same. He takes a few seconds to answer and comes out with, "That's okay with me, for now. I won't give up yet on a date though. Maybe we can hang out with your friend Alex at a game instead of going alone?" He looks so hopeful.

I smile brightly. This guy is really too sweet. I quickly accept, making Adam smile as well, big enough to show straight white teeth. The song switches to one with a faster pace. We continue to dance, and Adam is really a good dancer. I'm surprised I'm having such a great time after not wanting to come tonight. Alex gets my attention, and I pull Adam with me to go talk to her. I'm thirsty anyway, and I'm sure Adam is too by now.

When we reach her, I introduce Alex and Adam.

"Hey, Adam? Do you mind making sure Remi gets home safe? If that's alright with her?"

She directs the question at Adam but looks at me for my consent. Alex knows I won't mind getting home by myself. We'd planned walking or taking cabs home anyway since we've been drinking. "If you don't mind, Remi, I'm gonna take off with a friend."

"I'd be happy to see Remi home, Alex," Adam replies.

"Fine by me, Alex. I think we'll hang out a little longer, then we can probably walk back. I have some flats in my bag, and it's not too far back to the apartment." Alex hugs me goodbye, waves to Adam, and heads off to meet up with a guy with spiky black hair. I can't see much else about him as his back is turned, but he's dressed a little goth. Sort of punk rockerish. *So*, Alex's type. I get a text from Alex with the deets. It's our failsafe in case something happens so we know where the other was heading last. Something my dad always made us do. Leave a message with someone in the event something bad happens. If he'd only followed his own advice... Before I can get sidetracked by thoughts of my dad, I shake it off.

"I need some water and a drink, in that order," I say to Adam.

We make our way into the kitchen area with all the drinks and grab a couple cups. Adam fills his with beer off the tap, and I get a bottle of water for me out of a tub of ice. I decide on the drink with the red punch and bobbing fruit for after my water. After we fill our cups and we're heading out, in comes the guy that grabbed me earlier.

"Hi. I wanted to say sorry about earlier. I was hoping to find you to start again. My name's Christian. Should have probably led with that first instead of grabbing you." I accept his apology, and as I go to move around him he reaches out to grip my arm, stopping me. "Hey, I was wondering if you would still take me up on that dance." Fat chance, buddy, keep walking. There's something I don't really like about him. He makes my skin crawl.

"I'm going to just hang out a bit then head home with Adam. I'm danced out for now. Maybe next time?" I see a flash of irritation in his eyes, but he quickly covers it. As he turns, he knocks my drink out of my hand, spilling it.

"I'm so sorry. I didn't get any on you, did I? I think most of it went on me and the floor." Christian grimaces in apology like he didn't just do that on purpose.

He quickly grabs a towel and starts cleaning up, before walking over to the punch bowl to get me a new cup. I don't want to be obviously rude, but I'm not drinking anything from him. He excuses himself to the bathroom to cleanup. As soon as he's out of sight, I grab another cup.

I drink it steadily over the next little bit while visiting with Adam. I didn't realize how much alcohol was in that punch though. I hadn't smelled much in it.

"I think that drink is a little stronger than I thought it would be. I don't think I should have another of those," I tell Adam when he asks if I'd like another drink.

We meander around visiting with some other people Adam knows. I start to feel a little buzzed, and I'm getting tired. These heels, while sexy, are seriously starting to hurt. I ask Adam if he minds heading out soon. He agrees, and we go find our jackets in the front closet on the way out. I open my bag get to switch into the flats I slipped there earlier, but I wobble a little and have to brace myself on the wall when I step out of the heels.

"Here, let me help." Adam takes my shoes out of my hands, kneels down, and gently slides them on while I hold onto the wall for support. He pats my ankle a couple of times as he lets go, signaling he's done. He really is a nice guy, and I feel a little bad that I friendzoned him. After he stands up, we go to walk down the stairs, and it's at this point I'm really starting to feel out of it. "Remi, are you okay? You look a kinda spacey." Adam sounds concerned and a bit far away.

"I'm not sure. I didn't drink enough to get drunk, and I only drank what I got myself," I say with confusion at first.

I quickly come to the realization that I may have fallen for the most cliché college party crime. Unfortunately, Adam's next words confirm it.

"Oh crap, someone must have spiked the punch. Hey!" Adam yells at someone he knows, going in to get their attention. "I think the punch got spiked with something other than alcohol. Can you make sure no one else drinks it? And check in rooms and the yard for anyone that was drinking and may have passed out?" The guy agrees, saying he'll get some buddies to help, and hurries off to take care of it. "Remi, where do you live, sweetheart?" Adam pauses then says, "Or if you'd rather, I can take you back to my place."

I just want to get home to my room and hopefully Eli. Adam seems alright and nice, but I don't really know him.

"I'm staying at the Grayside building. Do you know where that is? I'm not sure I'll be able to walk there. I'm really not feeling well." Things are getting blurry, and sounds are starting to get far away. "Get my phone. Call Eli, please."

Adam pulling my phone out of my bag is the last thing I see before I pass out.

Adam

Hoping she's going to be okay, I fish Remi's phone out of her bag. This is not going to look good with her passed out, and I hope Eli doesn't freak out on me for it. If it wouldn't leave her alone, I would go find that piece of crap Christian. Finding Eli in the contacts, I hit the call button and listen as it starts to ring. Her friend will be super pissed at me too after she left her with me.

I try to think about how this conversation is going to go. I can't believe I was such an idiot and hope she doesn't blame me when she wakes up. The call goes to voicemail, and I hang up without leaving a message. If I didn't think she would freak out, I'd take her back to my place anyway, but she asked me to call a friend. After getting her over to one of the porch chairs and covered with her jacket I try the call again. If he doesn't pick up this time, I'll try her friend Alex. Finally, a voice on the other end picks up.

Chapter Six

Eli

My phone buzzes on the coffee table of my teammate's studio apartment where we're playing a video game. I glance at it and see that it's Remi. Silencing it, I go back to my game.

It starts buzzing again a few seconds later.

I ignore it.

I'm not going to be drunk dialed when she wants attention. We have to live together, and I'm sticking to my decision for her to make up her mind. Another drunk come on that I can't take advantage of is not my style. She can come to me when she's sober and in control of herself. She never would have told me that she was interested if I hadn't all but forced her into it.

She hasn't exactly been stringing me along, but it's been almost two months, and I feel like a douche that I kept pushing the issue. I have to consider that maybe she's too nice to say she isn't interested in anything romantic with me. Unfortunately, if she doesn't come to her own conclusion that we should be together, I don't think I can really be her friend. I'm too into her for that.

Disappearing as often as possible when I can't be in my room or class is the best course of action for now. Letting her take her time is wearing on me though as is keeping my hands to myself. The cooking lessons and dinners are hard to get through without touching her, and I'm getting a little irritated that it's taking so long for her to decide. I'm not exactly patient on the subject. She really is a great cook, and I could see her opening a café or doing something professional with it. I can't make myself not eat what she makes, so instead, I torture myself by sitting through those dinners. She has seemed on the verge of saying something several times, but so far she hasn't. I want her to be absolutely sure of her choice. I have no intention of letting her go once she chooses me, and I'm fairly certain that will eventually happen.

I feel like an angsty teenager with the thoughts running around my head. That girl has got me twisted up.

As my phone goes off again my friend Roger gestures towards it. "Hey man, you might wanna get that. What if something's wrong?"

"I doubt it, probably being drunk dialed." I don't want to let my buddy know what's going on, so I decide to answer it. Getting up and grabbing my phone, I pause the game and walk into the kitchen area.

"Hello?"

"Is this Elliot?" It's a male voice asking. Now I'm really irritated.

What the hell is going on that a guy is calling me from Remi's phone? Last I knew, her and Alex were going to a party. I get ready to hang up but decide to find out what the guy wants first.

"Where is Remi? Who is this, and why do you have her phone?" The words tumble out, worry making them harsh.

"This is Adam. Remi is passed out outside the sorority house. Someone put something in the punch the girls made, and she drank it. We were getting ready to leave, and she started feeling bad and crashed on the porch outside. Before she passed out, she asked me to call you. Can you tell me where to take her? She said she was staying at the Grayside building, but I don't know what apartment number she lives in. I offered to take her back to my place before, but she didn't want to do that. She said to call you instead. If you'd rather, I can take her to my place anyway."

Oh, hell no, he's not. She's coming home. Period.

And I'm going to go get her. I run back inside to grab my keys.

"Which sorority house are you at? I have my Jeep, so I'll come get you." Adam tells me where the house is and where they are outside. I can't believe I have to give her and her date a ride. I thought she was going with Alex, and my feelings are hurt, but I'm not about to leave her there.

"Roger," I say to my friend, "I need to go pick some people up. I'll see you later, man."

As I pull up I see a tall man about my height, and if I have to admit it, he's attractive from anyone's point of view. He's holding Remi propped up. Upon seeing me, he stands up with her bridal style, her long hair swinging free over his arm.

When I get close enough to see details, I realize I know him from the training team that takes care of the players. I'm trying to remember his name as I simultaneously tamp down on my raging jealousy.

Adam, that's his name.

I park and get out, going around the front to take Remi from him. During the transfer I make sure to keep her dress covering her perky ass. What little dress there is. She looks hot, and now I kinda feel bad for perving on her passed out body. He seems reluctant to let her go, and I can't say I blame him.

Since she seems to be breathing okay and sleeping soundly, I decide to take her home instead of the hospital. I get her buckled into the passenger seat and tell Adam to get in.

"Where do you want me to drop you?" I ask, looking into the mirror at him.

"I'll go with Remi. I don't think she should be alone until whatever she drank wears off." He says this like he's prepared to fight about it. Too bad she lives at my place. *Knew that had to come in handy at some point,* I think while trying to hide my grin.

"I'll keep an eye on her. She lives with me." I can't help the smirk that graces my lips and feel a sense of satisfaction, even it's wrong. Adam's gaze darts to mine with a quick inhalation and grimace. I sort of feel for the guy, but not enough to let him hang out with my unconscious girl.

"She didn't mention that she had a boyfriend. I didn't realize you were together." I can see he's working up the nerve to say something else. "She didn't say she was dating or living with anyone either, just for me to call you. You sure I don't need to stick around?"

Well, I guess that turns the tables on me. And I'm bit annoyed she didn't mention me at all. Maybe she doesn't consider us an 'us' at all?

If she doesn't, then I shouldn't either, and maybe I was being too harsh with this guy.

He did imply I might not be safe for her.

While that's plain bullshit, he could be a friend I've just not heard her mention. Like she didn't tell him about me…

"We're not dating, but it isn't for lack of trying on my part. Right now, we're temporary roommates, due to the flood at the dorms, and good friends. You really don't have to worry. I'll watch over her. Where to?"

I know I'm being rude, but I really don't care right now.

Adam reluctantly tells me where he lives, and I drop him off with his thanks. Before closing the door, he promises to check on Remi tomorrow.

Periodically, I glance over at Remi on the short drive home but don't notice anything odd or troubling.

I park in the garage and go around to pick her up out of the jeep, carrying her up the stairs. She stirs a little and wraps her arms around my neck. She sighs and mumbles about me smelling good, making me smile. She's still out of it and having a hard time keeping her grip on me. I wonder how coherent she actually is and if she knows where she's at. She's not too heavy, but three flights carrying another person is definitely good for the cardio. I could have taken the elevator but managing carrying her and working the lift gate would be a pain.

As I get her to her room, I balance her with one arm under her back and her bottom resting on my knee while I pull back her blankets and lay her down on the bed. I pull off her shoes and put her bag and heels I collected from Adam on the chair by the desk so she'll see them when she wakes up.

Getting a glass of water and some Tylenol, I leave them on the nightstand in case she ends up with a headache, before covering her up and brushing my lips across her forehead. I hear her trying to say something but can't quite make it out.

When I turn to leave, she says something else.

"Eli."

I'm not sure if she knows I'm here or she still thinks she's asking Adam to call me. Either way, I'm glad she turned to me when she needed help. Even if she only wants to remain friends. Turning to look back at her sleeping form before I close her door, I notice a large book on the desk. It's a *Complete Alice* illustrated book by Lewis Carroll. I've seen this book before; it's exactly like the one my roommate keeps on his dresser. I hope she hasn't been in there, although that's not something I would think she would do. I can ask her about it later or just go check it myself.

I go to one of my other roommate's room, and his book is still on his shelf proving she has the same one. It appears she hasn't even been in there. Feeling slightly guilty that I thought she was snooping around, I turn the light back out and head back to my room.

I get ready for bed, and right as I'm drifting off, I hear a thump and a curse. I'm up and out of my room, going down the hall still half asleep. Halfway down it I realize the noise came from Remi's room. Tapping lightly on the door before opening it, I peek in and then start to laugh. Looks like she got tangled in her blankets and fell off the bed.

"Hey, pretty girl, what are you doing on the floor?" I rub at my face to curb the laughter as well as to wake up some. When I glance down and look at her, her expression can only be described as wrathful. She shields her eyes from the hall light as she looks up at me.

"Eli? I feel like shit still. What the hell did I drink? I think I'm still feeling it for sure." I go scoop her up off the floor, blankets and all, and sit down on the bed with her in my lap. She rests her head on my shoulder and slides her arms around my chest, snuggling in. She grumbles, "You always smell so good. Why can't you be ugly or smell bad or something?"

I'm confused and trying to follow her train of thought.

"Yes, I'd definitely say you're still messed up, pretty girl. You're lucky I'm a gentleman, or I would be very tempted to take advantage of this situation," I tease as I brush her hair back from her face and kiss her forehead.

We sit for a few minutes in silence before she asks, "Eli, can you help me get out of this dress? It's not very comfortable, and I'd like to get something clean on."

I suck in a breath and stand us both up. Not how I imagined getting to undress her, but I can play friend for the night since that's what she needs. She can't stand very well, so I have her lean against me as I find the zipper in the back. As I lower it I don't think about the fact that I don't feel anything underneath in the area that there should be something.

I lean her back to help her off with it. It falls straight down, and I realize she's in my arms in only some lacy underwear that covers the edges of her ass cheeks. I close my eyes and groan.

This is so not happening right now. She speaks up, seeming unconcerned that I'm trying to avoid looking at her inappropriately.

"I need a shirt. Top drawer one of the cotton ones." She doesn't even seem to care that she's almost completely naked in front of me. I frown and wonder if that's normal for her or if she's comfortable with me. This woman is making me nuts. Never have I been this twisted up.

I go to the dresser and find a tank top, sleep shorts, and those fuzzy socks she loves. I grab a random pair and go to help her put it all on.

I get the top pulled over her head, regretting that I have to cover her up. Her chest isn't as large as some, but definitely more than average. High and firm, perfectly round where they hang with silver dollar sized dusky nipples. I want to drop my head down to them so badly that I bite my lip and glance away. When I look back up, her eyes are open, and she's staring at me with a small dazed smile on her face. I know I have to keep my hands, and other parts, to myself, but damn, this sucks. As I kneel in front of her I realize too late that was a bad idea. It brings me at eye level with the juncture of her thighs. I can see right through the lace of her panties, and I freeze with a sock in my hands. She's completely bare under them. I feel my pulse pick up as a decent volume of my blood hits my dick hard and croak out through a tight throat, "Remi, pick up your foot please. We need to finish getting you dressed. I'm going to do something inappropriate in about two seconds if I don't get you covered." She giggles a little and picks up a foot while holding onto the bedpost. She gets one then the other in the socks, and I quickly follow with pulling the shorts up. My fingers graze her bottom and thighs as I go, and I reluctantly release her after getting the shorts in place. Finally, I pick her up and settle her back in bed.

She lies down and closes her eyes as I cover her up. I'm getting ready to head back to my own bed, an act of sheer willpower at this point, when she throws an arm out toward me.

"Stay for a little bit?" Her words are still slightly slurred as she pats the bed behind her. I groan but suck it up and climb under the blanket with her.

This is testing the boundaries of my restraint. I pull her close, her back to my front. She sighs and snuggles in, wiggling her behind into my crotch. I tighten my hold to get her to stop. I think she's asleep when she says quietly, "Thank you for coming for me. Sorry I'm not more with it at the moment, I feel bad making you stay when things have been strained. I've been wanting to talk to you, but you keep avoiding me. Right now I have to sleep; I can't stay awake any more. Please tell me we'll talk soon."

I squeeze her again in answer and kiss the soft skin behind her ear before tucking her head under my chin and eventually dozing off with her.

Chapter Seven

Remi

I wake up with an insane headache.

What the heck happened last night? As I stretch and start to wake up, it all comes rushing back. Looking around, I see I'm in my bed and dressed in pajamas.

I didn't imagine it then.

Eli really was here. It's all mostly fuzzy. I see that the other pillow on my bed still has an imprint where he slept. I'm grateful he woke up early and took off before I could wake up and things got awkward. I see the pills and water on the table. Tossing back the pills I see on the table, I drain the glass and want more water. I get up and go into the bathroom, cringing when I see my reflection in the mirror.

Mascara is smeared around my eyes, and I have a major case of bed head going on. I start the water in the shower, chugging another glass from the tap while it's heating. I find the silver dress from last night on the chair, and after checking it for stains, hang it up. I'll have to take it to the dry cleaners on my next shopping trip. I strip, toss my clothes in the hamper, and step into the shower. The water feels great on my skin, and after I wash up, I just stand in the stream of it for a while.

Finally, it starts to cool, and I drag myself out to dry off. I wrap my hair in a towel and go into my room to get dressed in some comfortable sweats and a tank top. As I'm pulling on some purple and pink fuzzy socks there's a knock on the door. Assuming it has to be Eli as we're the only ones here, I yell for him to come in.

"Hey, how are you feeling?" he asks, not moving from the doorway.

"Better after a shower and the Tylenol. Thanks for leaving that for me." I feel awkward sitting on the unmade bed and making small talk.

"Yeah, figured you'd have a headache. So, what happened? I didn't think you would leave your drink unattended or take one from someone you didn't know." He gives his condemnation in an accusatory tone, and I try not to get defensive. It *was* kind of stupid to drink out of the punch bowl.

"I think the rum punch the girls made must have gotten spiked with something. It was fine earlier in the night. I should have just had a beer out of the tap instead. I feel like a dumb ass about it for sure." I bite my lip before asking my next question, not wanting to bring it up but needing to know. "What happened with Adam?" I hold eye contact as I ask. I hope this isn't going to be too uncomfortable, but I'm not going to shy away like I did something wrong either.

"I dropped him off at his place before I brought you back here and got you into bed. I thought you went out with Alex last night?" Again, with the accusing tone. "I didn't expect to find some guy stuck to you with Alex nowhere around. Adam wanted to stay with you, but I wasn't sure what the situation was, and frankly, I didn't want to bring him back here. He said you never mentioned that you were dating anyone when I said that I'd stay with you." He looks half hurt and half pissed, giving me a narrow look.

This is so not going well.

I start working my hair up into a ponytail to give my hands something to do besides fidget.

"He didn't seem too happy about it either, so I told him you were my roommate. What happened to you not being interested in dating right now, Remi? Isn't that what you told me?" Eli grits the last out with his jaw tight.

He's pissing me off. I understand him being upset, but I'm not going to sit and take the attitude. I try to calmly gather what I want to say. I'm not sure where this conversation is going, but I know I don't want to alienate Eli further. I really do like him, and I'll eventually, in my own time, get around to showing him that. I just haven't been ready to take the chance on something serious evolving yet until I was sure that's what I wanted. After last night, I can no longer deny to either of us that I want him. And I'm going to have to get up the courage to say so before he decides he doesn't want *me* any longer. I decide to be completely honest and not leave anything out even though I don't feel I should have to explain myself.

"I did go out with Alex; she's the one that wanted to go to the party, not me. I would have rather been doing what you were and staying in. I met Adam while I was at the party. He rescued me from a jerk with wandering hands, and we danced and talked some. We ran into the same guy again a little later while we were getting drinks, and he introduced himself that time and asked me out. I turned him down, and he left, knocking my drink over, supposedly on accident, on his way out of the room. I think he did it on purpose, and he got me another drink." Eli starts to say something, but I hold my hand up. I'm not finished yet. "I took it but didn't drink it. I dumped it out as soon as he left, got a new cup, and filled it myself. It had to have already been in the drink at that point. Alex had asked earlier if I was okay with Adam walking me home so she could go with a friend. I actually have a class with Adam; that's how he knew who I was. I didn't know his name, but he seemed nice. I also hope he doesn't think badly of me after I passed out on him as I actually like him. As a friend." I laid it all out as concise and straightforward as possible.

I knew I had to be careful, or I was going to push him away without much effort. He'd been avoiding me before, but now the space between us felt different, strained. I didn't want him to give up on me; I only wanted more time to figure things out. I start to panic at the thought, but Eli's next words bring me back to reality quickly.

"Seriously, Remi? You practically give yourself a mickey, and you're worried what some douche will think about you?" I don't think that's quite fair to Adam, but I'll keep my mouth shut for the moment. "You could have gotten hurt. What if he wasn't a good person? You don't have to worry though," he says, his tone changing with his words, "he knew you were drugged right away. He said you told him to call me." The last is said with a raised brow, so I answer it.

"He's nice and was interesting. We hung out, and I'm embarrassed about what happened." Before I can continue, he starts talking again.

"Why are you worried what he thinks? Again, I thought you weren't interested in dating or is that only if it pertains to me?" he says venomously, obviously not liking that I was interested in another dude. "Why didn't you go with him instead of coming back here?" he asks with his arms crossed. I don't think I'm going to get anywhere with him being so confrontational, but I try anyway.

"Eli, of course I would come back here. I wasn't going to go stay with some guy I only met a few hours ago." At that, Eli makes a rude noise and gets a dirty look in return. "Just because he was nice to me and shares a class with me doesn't mean he's safe. And why would you think I'd take off with someone else when I'm hung up on you? What is wrong with you? Thank you for getting me and taking care of me. I really appreciate it, but I don't know what I've done to upset you so badly other than hang out with someone with a penis that's not you. I asked him to call you, for fuck's sake. I could have had him call Alex or even gone home with him!"

Now I'm yelling and blurting out everything that pops into my head. This is going all wrong, but he's making me so angry I really want to smack him.

"You think of me when you want to be safe?" he asks quietly. His anger is noticeably absent, and he has a hopeful look in his eyes. Me, not so much. I'm still furious. With a blooming grin, his next question pushes me back to exasperated. "How hung up are you?"

"Really? That's the part you focus on? Not the irrational jealousy, well, maybe a *little* rational, but still." I'd have been pissed about that too if the situation were reversed, but I'm not letting him off that easily. This is getting dealt with now, and boundaries are being defined.

"Remi, I came out and all but asked you to be my girlfriend, and instead of telling me straight up that you don't want me, you drag it out. Hanging out with me and my friends, letting me be the only one trying for more. If you only wanted to be friends, you should have said so. I wouldn't have held it against you. I would have been your friend. Then I think that you do want me, but you're just not ready, so I back off.

Now it seems the first guy you see at a party you grab onto with both hands. You're here right now, and I have to see you every day, and I can't say anything to you or touch you without it possibly being inappropriate because of this situation of you being my fucking roommate for god's sake. That would be beyond taking advantage if I came off as pushing you into something so you'll have a place to stay, so I backed off. I need to know where I stand. Friends, not friends.. more if that's possible after this conversation. Just tell me, please." Eli had started out yelling, and now he's down to a quieter frustrated level. I know whatever I say next will decide how our relationship is from now on, and I aim to get it right.

"Elliot, I never meant to be indecisive. I'm not sure that I'm ready for anything serious. That's why I wouldn't go out one on one with you. I enjoy being around you; I like you, period. All the likes are really making me feel like I'm in high school by the way. Also, there are things that you don't know, things that I don't know if I'm ready to share..." I trail off with a sigh.

"That's it? That's your only issue?" he asks. Getting closer to me, he takes my face in his hands. They're a little rough, but not as much as you'd think for an athlete.

"Yes, I-I want to try. If you still do, that is," I whisper.

At that, he closes the distance, and our lips meet. Soft yet steady. I put my hands on his forearms. He turns his head slightly, parting his lips. As I mimic him, he slides his tongue into my mouth. With a catch in his breath, his hands slide into my hair, his fingers tangling in the strands. It feels electric, and I slide my hands up to his shoulders, gripping tight. Deciding to flow with the change, I slip my tongue out to meet his. That's all he needs to increase the depth as one hand drifts down to my hip, pulling me tight to his body. A fluttering starts in my abdomen where I'm pressed against his lower body, and I can tell exactly how this is affecting Eli. A soft noise starts in my throat as I rock my hips against his. Before it can go any further, he pulls back, giving me a couple slow pecks on the lips then resting his forehead against mine.

I can hear the smile in his voice as he says, "This I can work with." With that cryptic remark, he pulls away and backs out of my room.

I touch my lips, stunned at the plethora of emotions running through me. Hot and cold, up and down. I'm slightly exhausted after that emotional roller coaster.

Too bad we couldn't have just jumped straight to the end there. It would have been so much easier than all the hurt feelings and confusion. I feel a lot was left out, and I'm a bit unclear on how point A made it to point B of being okay, but I'll chalk it up to a guy thing. If he's happy with it, I will be too. What I really need is one of those big red EASY buttons you see on commercials.

I shake my head to clear my thoughts out and grab my school bag, deciding to pull out some assignments to complete for classes next week. I sit down at the desk and get started with the thought that while I don't know where we're going, I think I just might enjoy the ride.

Later that afternoon I hear a buzzer ringing and voices coming from down the hallway. I come out of my room to see what's going on. As I enter the living area I see Adam talking to Eli and hear him asking after me. Eli tries to tell him I'm resting, but right then Adam looks up and sees me. A big smile breaks out on his face, and Eli scowls and heads for the couch. I hide my laugh behind my hand, turning it into a cough when he shoots me a glare. I don't think he appreciates me laughing at him at the moment. I turn my attention to Adam as he speaks.

"Remi, glad to see you're looking better. I was hoping you were alright after last night. I feel terrible about it. I came by to see how you're feeling." Adam comes close, and I reroute for the opposite side of the couch that Eli is on, leaving Adam to take the chair or the loveseat since I'm guessing that he won't take the middle seat between us. I feel like choosing a seat was a diplomatic exercise and refrain from rolling my eyes.

"Much better, thank you for calling Eli. I appreciate you taking care of me; I'm not sure a lot of the guys at that party would have. Or would have in a much different way." I'm grateful for his help and try to convey that without giving either of them the wrong impression.

"Not a problem." He looks over at Eli then back to me, clearly uncomfortable with what he wants to say, but he squares his shoulders and asks, "So, do you think you feel up for a movie tonight? And maybe some dinner?" Should have seen that was coming. Ugh, awkward. Seems like that's going to be the word for the day.

I try to glance at Eli to gauge his reaction without making it obvious. "Umm...I'm not sure. Eli, did you have any plans for tonight?" I drop the not so subtle hint. I think that's mostly clear on both sides without being completely obvious about it.

"I was thinking about continuing the COD tournament with some friends since I didn't go back last night, but after this morning I wasn't sure what I'd be doing." He gives me a look as if challenging me to say something to contradict his allusion. Wisely, I keep my mouth shut, and he directs the rest to Adam. "Although I'm surprised you'd think Remi was up to going out so soon after getting drugged last night." Eli turns with a dark look aimed at an indignant Adam. I knew he wouldn't pass up a chance to make the guy look bad. Adam just ignores him and addresses me.

"Well, actually, I kind of picked a few movies and thought we could order something in. Here or my place, wherever you'd be more comfortable. If you'd like to, that is," he finishes on a fast exhale.

I can tell he's nervous. He had a good answer too. Can't really see where Eli could fault him for that. Staying on Eli's turf and being conscientious that I might not be up for much.

And…the point goes to Adam. Not that I'm keeping track. Wait, I totally am.

Adam is still waiting on me to say something. I feel like I'm one wrong step from them both whipping it out and marking me like I'm a bitch in heat. Trying to hide my grin, I snicker at the visual. Both guys look at me like I might be a little screwy. Oh well, I probably am. I finally come out with a mostly diplomatic answer.

"Eli, if it's okay with you, I wouldn't mind staying here and vegging out over a movie and some pizza. You wanna stay in too, or are you going out?" I keep my gaze in his direction with my brows raised in question.

In my peripheral I see Adam shoot me a surprised look. I'm not sure if it's for the invite to Eli or the fact that I took him up on his movie night. I can see how he might not have expected me to invite Eli, but he can't really say anything as it's not his place to regulate my friends or even his house we'll be at. Eli can stay if he wants to. I can tell he's hoping Eli will say no, but of course, Eli says he'd be happy to stay in and offers to grab some pizza menus out of the kitchen, calling back to us to ask if either of us has a preference on which pizza place to order from.

"I'll be right back. I didn't want to be presumptuous and bring my bag up." Adam excuses himself to run downstairs and is back in a few minutes. "I have a bunch of choices since I didn't know what you'd like."

He pulls out several new releases covering horror, action, sci-fi, and romantic comedy. *Holy cow, he's really going all out with the sweetheart routine.* He couldn't go wrong with all those choices to choose from.

"Blood and guts, it is," I proclaim as I snag the horror flick from the pile. "We can do the romantic comedy when we get sleepy," I say with a laugh. Rom coms are for girls night as far as I'm concerned.

Eli grabs some throw blankets out of a closet, and Adam helps him move the coffee table off to the side while still leaving it close enough to the giant pillows we opted to use as chairs so that we'll be able to reach everything. I put the movie in as Adam goes back downstairs and gets the door when the delivery buzzes and he pays for the pizza. Eli comes in with paper plates, napkins, and drinks for us all. We all get settled on the floor with our food as the movie starts.

Partway through, I'm glued to the screen as victim number four or maybe five gets eaten by the alien when I feel an arm slide in behind my shoulders. Well, crap, this isn't awkward at all. I start to stiffen and instead choose to ignore it for now and enjoy the movie. Thankfully, Eli doesn't notice, or if he does, he doesn't make a fuss about it. After the first movie ends, I tell the boys to pick the next one and jump up to make some popcorn. I put it in two large bowls and put one on either side of me, so no one has to stretch any body parts to get to it. Before I sit back down, I adjust my pillow and blanket in a way that would make it quite obvious if Adam tried putting his arm back around me. Hopefully, it's enough to dissuade him. The third popcorn bowl in the middle should also help everyone keep hands in their own bubbles. Eli pushes play on the action film, and we all settle in to watch it.

Before long, Eli stretches out near my feet and starts to play with my socks, tracing the lines of the designs on them. Of course he can't keep quiet for the duration of Adam's visit.

"By the way, Remi, I found one of your fuzzy socks in my room. You must have left it in there. Or I suppose maybe in the dryer and it accidentally ended up in my basket." He throws that out there all nonchalantly, the little shit.

I freeze. Well, now the points are even. Nice one, Eli, like that wasn't meant to make it seem like I took them off in there in the first place, even with your little disclaimer. I'm annoyed enough that I give it to him right back with an evil little grin while staring directly at the tv.

"I'm sure it has nothing to do with your weird little foot fetish, and it's more likely you accidentally didn't put them back after borrowing them." Next to me, Adam chokes on his popcorn but wisely keeps quiet. My chest is shaking with my suppressed mirth. I hear Eli mutter "touché," and with that, he starts to rub my feet. I let out an involuntary noise at a particular spot that's still sore from the heels last night and stiffen when I realize it.

Normally, I wouldn't worry about any of this with friends or strangers around, but these two have me reconsidering everything I do so I don't offend either one of them. I'm getting more and more uncomfortable between the two men.

Eli, yes, I can admit I am interested in. Adam? Not so much in that way. I really like him, but as friend material only. Now I have to figure out how to box him firmly back into the friendzone without hurting his feelings, and before Eli does anything else to mark his territory. Like a hickey. My boss would kill me.

I scrunch up my face at that thought. Just, no. I can't afford to be benched until it fades. The idea of Eli being that possessive really doesn't scare me like I thought it would though, which is quite the surprise to me.

In the middle of the third movie I begin to nod off. The boys must think I'm asleep because I hear them shut it off and move into the kitchen. They quietly begin to talk, and I unashamedly eavesdrop.

"So," I hear Adam begin. "Did I misunderstand the situation last night? Are you two together?"

I'm kicking myself for saying Eli and I were just friends. It's complicated, but I didn't have to make it seem like I was single and lead Adam on even if that wasn't my intention.

"Not so much together, more so seeing where it goes. She says she's not ready for anything serious, and I'm okay with waiting until she is. Is tonight an indication I need to be worried about you?" *Well, that was straight and to the point.* Good for him being all mature after his earlier actions.

Adam takes a moment to respond.

"I like her. She didn't even know I existed until I introduced myself last night. Was dumb luck some idiot frat boy decided to get handsy and I got the chance to step in. Not that I was happy someone being a dick was an opportunity for me; that came out wrong. She's been in several of my classes for almost two months but never even noticed me." He's makes a sad kind of huffing sound, like he's calling himself an idiot. I sort of feel bad. "I only brought up the one class since I didn't want to feel like a complete fool, but she did at least say I looked familiar. I'm not sure if that was to spare my feelings or not. I also can't say I don't want to try for more. I won't push her about it or infringe if she's already spoken for; that's not my style. I would like to at least be her friend, and I do intend on doing that just so that you're aware." He says it almost as a challenge, and when Eli doesn't take the bait, he continues. "I've been interested since I first saw her."

Three classes? Four? I'm still drawing a blank other than he truly does look familiar. Now I really do feel bad.

"It's not my place to say who is or isn't her friend, but I'll warn you now, don't play with her." I think I'm warming up to Eli's protective attitude. It's sorta nice in a Neanderthal way.

Finally, I hear them say their goodnights, and a few moments later the door closes. As I start drifting off, I'm vaguely aware of Eli moving around, putting food away, cleaning up, and turning out lights. I hear him come close and sit down. By now I'm barely awake and content just to stay here in the giant pillow nest.

"Hey, baby doll. You want help getting to bed?" All he gets for his effort is a grunt. Super ladylike, I know, but I'm just too tired to care. "I can carry you if you'd prefer. These pillows are comfortable now but won't be if you roll off onto the floor. I've done it a time or two." I can hear the smile in his voice. He sounds happy. Without cracking an eye, I hold an arm straight up and wait for him to guide it around his neck. "I'll take that as I'm your chariot then."

He picks me up like I weigh as much as one of those pillows and heads down the hallway. I'm thinking I don't mind being carried by my big football player when wham! Head bounces off the corner of the turn in the hall he didn't quite navigate properly.

"Son of a—what the hell, Eli!" I grumble as I open one eye far enough to glare at him while rubbing my head. Did he really just bounce my head off the wall? Such a dork. He instantly starts apologizing.

"Crap, Remi, are you okay? I'm so sorry. Hold on, let me get you in your room and then I'll check it," he says as he continues carrying me down the hallway. When we get to my room, he sets me down on the bed and instantly looks at my eyes then starts to gently rub through my hair, looking for a bump. As he finds it, I hiss in air. "Go in the bathroom and get ready for bed. I'll get you some more Tylenol." Sounding frustrated, he leaves the room. I'm sure he feels bad about the attempted concussion, and I start to giggle until it makes me grab my head with a wince.

I ignore his orders and get up. I'm awake now and ready to get into pajamas. Some soft and loose short shorts with polka dots and a plain cotton tank top. Tossing my bra in the closet, I adjust my socks and head into the bathroom. I pull a wide wrap band around my head to keep my hair back and coat my face and neck in minty face cream. I rinse my hands and get my toothbrush and paste out and start brushing my teeth. As I do, I see a movement in my peripheral and turn to see Eli standing there with his hands suspended, pills in one and a glass of water in the other, taking me in from head to toe. At least the face cream is hiding my blush unless the heat I can feel creeping across my chest gives me away.

"Never seen a girl wash her face and brush her teeth before?" I mumble around a mouthful of foam. Oh, good going, now your spit is dripping down your chin. Teach me to talk with my mouth full.

That thought nearly causes me to choke as I think of other things a mouth could be full of. I must have hit my head harder than I thought to meander that far down the gutter from basic hygiene.

From the look on Eli's face, he may also have been thinking along the same lines as I was.

"I like the shorts…" With a perusal from my toes to my chest, then finally up to meet my gaze with a dirty grin, he finishes, "And the top." I look down and see my nipples have hardened from the cool air in the room and are showing through the thin material of my tank.

Attempting to break the sexual tension going on, I toss out, "It's cold in here, or is that only a guy excuse?" I snigger, more at the awfulness of the joke than the joke itself, but it does the job. Eli laughs, and the mood breaks. He brings the pain reliever and the water into the bathroom and places them on the counter. I spit and bend down to rinse my face and hear a quick inhale of air behind me and a soft groan, with a muttering of, "You've got to be freaking kidding me." I raise my eyes to the mirror and see Eli's are situated decidedly lower than face height. I probably should have considered the absence of length on the shorts.

Deciding to own it, I shrug and finish rinsing my face and neck and dry them off while Eli continues to watch me. I picture thanking him for his assistance, telling him goodnight, and climbing into bed with a smile on my face as I drift off. Well, it probably could have gone that way yesterday. Instead, Eli scoops me up and carries me across the room before following me down onto the bed. I keep my arms looped around his neck, so he can't escape.

"So, do I get a snuggle buddy again? I think I'm owed time since you did take off on me this morning." I arch an eyebrow in challenge as I wait for his reply, dropping my arms when he pulls back.

He rubs the back of his neck while contemplating his reply. "I wasn't sure how much you would remember, and I didn't want you to think I was a perv that takes advantage when you're not coherent."

I look at him in surprise, aghast that he would think I would take it that way.

"I would never think that. Even if I didn't remember, I know you wouldn't do something like that. And I kind of remember, but it's mostly hazy. I do vaguely remember you carrying me and helping me change, then being snuggled and warm. That's about it. If I did anything else, say of the embarrassing nature, I haven't a clue," I add on just to cover my bases.

"Actually, that's mostly accurate. Not too bad for the la la land you were in. Other than having no modesty. Not that I can say I mind, just maybe don't drink random things next time so I can enjoy it. Does that mean I get to sleep with you again?" He gives me expectant eyes. I nod, and he gets up and starts stripping. I laugh and throw a pillow at him that he catches.

"Go brush your teeth and come back. I'll keep it warm." I tuck in under the blankets, getting comfortable while Eli grabs his toothbrush from his bathroom, and he comes back in a t-shirt and pajama pants. Kind of cute that he came back in here to brush his teeth instead of doing it in his own bathroom. Maybe he was afraid I'd change my mind.

I hear the water start then he asks, "I saw the Alice book on your desk, mind if I ask where you got it?" My brain stutters to a halt. I see it every day, and it's a bittersweet reminder of a beautiful boy I used to know. I keep it short and to the point.

"It was a gift from an old friend."

I think that's the end of it when I don't hear a reply at first.

"Huh, my roommate has the same one. So random that you have one too. I catch him reading it sometimes. We all give him shit over it." Eli laughs a bit about it, but I find it adorable. It's one of my favorite collections.

"I have more by the same author, but they're in storage. That one's my favorite." I've become super drowsy, and the last thing I hear is Eli using the mouth rinse in my bathroom.

I fall asleep before he gets back; I must have been more tired than I thought. I snuggle into him when he climbs in, breathing in the minty smell of the toothpaste mixed with the combination of other products he uses and his own smell.

Guys always have such good scents.

I sigh and slide back into sleep as he kisses the top of my head and pulls me closer.

Chapter Eight

On Monday, school is just dragging on. The professors give out so many assignments I'm going to be busy every night this week just to keep up. It makes for an all around crappy day.

I woke up by myself.

Again.

What is up with him sneaking out before I'm awake? I make a stop at the grocery store on the way back to the house. As I come in through the automatic doors, I see Adam checking out at a stand. I groan internally, not wanting to deal with any of his drama today. I only need a few things for dinner and some personal hygiene things, and then I can go back home.

The cause that I need those for could be part of my problem.

I'll have to make sure to keep the trash under the sink for the next few days. Not that I'm embarrassed, but it can be a little awkward with a guy that you're sorta/not quite dating to see if he happens to go into your bathroom.

I wave to Adam as I pass without slowing down. He looks like he wants to come over, but he's in the middle of checking out and can't exactly follow me without leaving his item. I hurry and grab what I need and head for the express lane. I don't see Adam, so he must have taken off. I answer the usual greetings from the clerk with a smile and swipe my card while she bags up my few items.

As I get out to the parking lot and see him waiting outside my car, I start to get annoyed. He starts talking before I quite reach him, before I can even say anything.

"How'd the rest of your weekend go? I would have called, but I didn't want you to think I was stalking you." Adam looks nervous and unsure of his welcome with his hands in his jeans pockets. I must still have the grumpy look on. I make an effort to put on a pleasant expression as I unlock my car and place my purchases in the backseat floorboard. Straightening up, I turn to address him.

"It was good. Just caught up on schoolwork. Not that you can tell now. Every class just gave me twice as much as last week. I'm going to be working on it non-stop." I move around to my door and stand in the opening. "I've got to get going, still have dinner to make." I gesture to the bags in the back. "See you in class tomorrow?"

He smiles now. Not so nervous anymore.

"I'll save you a seat. See you tomorrow, Remi."

With a wave he walks to a later model blue truck while I get in my car and head for home.

At home I make baked chicken, mashed potatoes, and heat up some beans out of a can in between reading assignments. With the college prep courses I took and the community college I completed, I have about three semesters left to finish my degree in business management. It's a shorter degree, but I wasn't positive what I wanted a career in, and it can really be applied in a multitude of ways. If there's something else I decide I want to do, a lot of the classes are stepping stones for other majors.

Thinking of high school and what happened my senior year and directly after, puts me in an even worse mood than my period already has.

Eli comes in shortly after dinner is done and heads straight for it.

"This is fantastic. What am I going to do when you leave me?"

"Fend for yourself maybe?" I snap out.

He could have said hello first. It may be irrational, but I'm annoyed he went for the food first, then I'm annoyed that I'm annoyed. I huff a breath in frustration at myself.

I decide to pack up my work and take it to the desk in my room. I'm getting a headache anyway, and there's no point sticking around to be grumpy with Elliott.

"Everything okay?" he asks cautiously. I see him looking around, trying to figure out if he actually did something wrong or not.

"Peachy. I have work to do, so I'm going to take this to my room since I'm not the greatest company. I'll clean up dinner in a little bit."

With that, I move my work to my room and spread it over my desk. For the next while, I do my best to absorb what I'm reading, so I can write a paper on it. I hear Eli moving around in the kitchen, and a few minutes later there's a quick knock on the door before he opens it.

He brought me a plate of food.

Setting it down on an empty corner of the desk, he retreats out the door and back down the hall. I take a break and eat, then take my plate to the kitchen. He's cleaned up the whole dinner mess. I rinse my plate and put it in the dishwasher. Without seeing Eli anywhere, I head back to my desk to finish up my homework.

A little while later, I feel him come up behind me and begin rubbing my shoulders and neck. Oh, that feels good. I drop my chin down to my chest as the tension leaves me.

Eli leans in and murmurs in my ear, "Let's go do something, get out of this apartment."

For a minute, I debate on continuing with my homework then decide to go with him. I'm not going to get much else done right now anyway.

I throw on some tennis shoes and pull my favorite soft, maroon leather jacket on over my t-shirt. Occasionally, I get to take home clothes from shoots, and this was from one of those jobs last year. I double check my appearance in the closet mirror, making sure I'm presentable for public. Well broken in jeans that are comfortable and hug all the right places and a bit of a dressy tee with a v neck and some gathers to make it fitted.

It'll do as long as we don't go anywhere too fancy. I grab my wallet and keys and tuck them in my jacket pockets.

Eli is coming out of his room dressed similarly in jeans and a t-shirt with his own leather on. His is black, so at least we're in different colors.

I do have to say his jeans are looking mighty nice, and I can see all the definition under his shirt. I stare for a moment, and when I look up, I realize I got caught checking him out.

Again.

He has a self-satisfied grin on his face. I make a scowl at him and turn to leave, and together we go down the stairs. Instead of heading outside, he turns, and I follow him to a door I haven't been through. As we walk in, I see we're in the garage. There's his Jeep, but he heads around that and instead goes to a sleek monster of a motorcycle.

"This is yours?" I ask with a hint of disbelief.

"No, it's my roommates. He won't mind if we take it out." He puts on a full helmet and holds another out to me. It's déjà vu. The back of my eyes burn, and I must look as stricken as I feel. Eli notices and flips his visor up. Setting aside the other helmet, he takes my hand. "Remi, what's wrong?"

I try to compose myself. Stupid hormones.

"I'm fine. I just used to know someone that had a bike just like this. It was a surprise seeing it is all." I shake off the feelings and reach for the helmet, mustering up a smile. There's no reason to dwell on the past; I intend to enjoy this. I came here to get on with my plans after all the mess with my dad, and I don't plan to deviate from my course.

"If you want to talk about it, we can skip this and stay in." I give him a look. The one that indicates he should drop it. "Or we could just talk later. Get up here, and I'll show you how to sit." He looks like he's going to say more, but he thinks better of it.

I give a small smile, grateful for the subject being dropped.

Shaking off my melancholy, I smirk up at him and throw my leg over the seat and slide into place, fitting my feet into the holds. I sink into his back and put my hands on his hips.

"Well, I guess I don't need to help you after all," Eli says with some surprise. I laugh a little and nudge him to get going. He pulls his visor back down and starts the bike. It fires up with a roar. I slide my arms snugly around his waist as he calls back, "Hang on," and pulls out of the garage.

We ride into town, going through it and out the other side then continuing down the highway until we're on the outskirts of the next town over. I can smell fall in the air, the crisp wind and loamy mix of dirt and wilting leaves as we get out into the country.

It's just beautiful.

I'm having such a good time that I could stay like this forever. The turning leaves on the trees look like they're on fire as they're illuminated by the sun on its descent. Eventually, Eli slows and turns down a paved road. As we come around the curve in the road I see it opens up onto a farm.

Pumpkins!

There's a sign giving directions to the various attractions, a corn maze lit up with flood lights, and a tractor with hay bales driving people around. I see a stall with both food and crafts for sale and am so excited I can barely wait for Eli to find a place to park and get his helmet off. Mine is already off, and I'm finger combing my hair. He stores our helmets and pushes my hands out of the way, smoothing it down for me. I feel my stomach flip on the spot. He really is such a great guy and I'm insanely lucky to have him so into me. I grab his hand and turn to the lane leading to the pumpkins, pulling him behind me in my excitement.

"Oh my god, I haven't been to an autumn festival in years!" I almost knock Eli over as I stop abruptly and throw my arms around his chest to hug him tight.

He catches me and smiles down into my face. He's always attractive but so sexy when he smiles. I realize I really want this, want *him*. I reach up and slowly touch his lips with mine, keeping eye contact the whole time. His eyes darken as he slides his hand down to clutch at my hip. I feather a couple more kisses over his mouth and settle back down on my heels. Grabbing his hand again, I pull his slightly stunned self behind me and make a beeline for a caramel apple stand.

I notice the attention we're getting with Eli holding my hand in line. He's getting eye fucked by women young and old alike. With his size and looks, I suppose they'd have to be dead not to notice him. I hook my arm through his, effectively staking my claim, and continue to wait in line.

After we get our apples we walk over to the pumpkin patch, meandering through the paths.

"I don't think we can get a pumpkin on the bike though," I tell Eli a little wistfully as I eye the pumpkins. "I can come back another day in my car."

"Maybe pick a few smaller ones, and we can tuck them in the saddlebags." I smile brightly at the suggestion and continue searching through the patch for my perfect pumpkins. He chuckles at my enthusiasm and just follows along.

We pick two smaller ones and go pay for them at the stall. Eli volunteers to run them to the bike while I browse the stalls. There's a beautiful woven purple scarf I'm admiring when hands go over my eyes. I smile and turn around, dislodging the hands. As I look up I lose my smile.

Christian is standing there.

"Fancy meeting you here, gorgeous."

I repress the full body shudder that tries to overtake me as he speaks. This guy is a serious fuckwad. I throw a glare at him as I move a few steps away.

"Hello, Christian."

I begrudgingly greet him as I look around for Eli as unobtrusively as possible and see he's almost to us.

I'm relieved he's close.

I'd hate to show that I can protect myself if I don't have to. Better to save that as a surprise if he gets out of hand and actually manages to catch me alone. He must see where I'm looking and tries to grab my elbow saying, "Let's go do the corn maze." I shake his hand off me as Eli reaches us and slides an arm around my waist, pulling me back out of Christian's reach.

Almost an exact repeat of when Adam interfered the other night. The similarity isn't lost on Christian, and his face darkens into a scowl.

"Collect men everywhere you go don't you, gorgeous?" His voice is low and not pleased with the interference.

No, not pleased at all.

I get goosebumps from the nastiness I feel emanating from him. Guy seriously has a problem being turned down. I decide if he continues to harass me, I'll go to the school's admin to report him.

"I do believe we were just heading off to the maze, weren't we, darling?" Eli replies in a careful voice. I can hear the underlying threat. If I don't get him away from Christian soon, there's going to be an altercation. Eli is usually insanely sweet, but at the moment I'm not sure he wouldn't pulverize the creep. His fingers tighten on my hip almost painfully until I wiggle and he loosens his hold immediately. I don't think that will go over well for Eli with football or his scholarship. Not that Christian wouldn't deserve it, but I don't want Eli jeopardizing his status with this idiot.

To diffuse the situation, I begin maneuvering in the other direction with Eli and turn my head to speak as we walk away.

"Yes, I do believe we were. Goodbye, Christian, have a good evening."

With that, I turn back to face the direction we're going, surprised I didn't trip already.

We walk away towards the maze.

"That was the guy from the party the other night, the one that Adam was talking about?" Eli has a concerned look on his face now that he's addressing me. I wiggle my hips a little, bumping into him, to catch his attention. His hand is still clamped around mine like I might try to escape or be pulled away. "Sorry, babe, I hope I didn't bruise you." He starts rubbing little distracting circles on the skin of my hip with his thumb. He's such a touchy feely guy, and I like it.

"Yes, the one Adam helped with when I first got there, then again when he spilled my drink later on." Eli's face hardens with anger.

"He's got a hard on for you. Try to steer clear of him. I've heard rumors about him and girls, but I didn't realize at the time that it was him. I'm sure he spiked the punch knowing you wouldn't take a glass from him. He's second string on the team and has been in some questionable situations but always manages to get out of it. If anything is ever proven, he'll be booted immediately."

"Let's not worry about him right now. He's a creep, and I'll be sure to stay away from him. I just want to enjoy tonight. You made excellent plans, and I won't let him ruin them. Let's do this maze then go get some cider and find a hay bale on that tractor over there."

I point in the direction of the tractor ride, and when Eli turns his head to follow my finger, I give into the urge and lean up on my toes to peck him on the cheek, getting pricked a little by his stubble. I use the distraction to take off ahead of him for the maze. He laughs as he chases after me. We take several wrong turns, and at each dead end where we find ourselves alone Eli steals a quick kiss. After the third dead end, I'm getting frustrated with the teasing brushing of lips. When he goes to pull back this time, I loop my arms around his neck and deepen the kiss instead, prolonging it until I'm satisfied. Eli gives me that devious little smile of his as we break apart, and I'm slightly breathless.

He knows exactly what he's been doing, and I fell for it.

I decide I still got what I was after, shrug good naturedly, and continue on with a pat to his tight rear as I pass him. Finally, we find our way through the maze, and Eli follows through on my request, buying us both steaming cups of cider at a vendor booth. It sounded good earlier, but after playing in the maze and getting hot in more than one way, something cold and better yet alcoholic would have been nice right about then.

I take my cup, and we move into the line for the hay-ride. The tractor is just coming back around to drop off and pick up new passengers. Eli holds my cup while I climb on, and I return the favor. We find a bale big enough for us both to sit on with two more stacked behind that make a nice place to lean back and enjoy the ride snuggled up together. Eli gently strokes my hair, wrapping it around his finger before letting it spiral back off and then repeating the motions. I sigh and rest my head on his shoulder, perfectly content. I feel his other hand slip up the front of my shirt then down under the waistband of my jeans. His thumb starts brushing lightly over the crest of my hipbone causing a jolt of heat to streak through me. I wiggle and quietly hum my appreciation, hoping no one noticed. Eli definitely has talented hands, barely having to put them on me to elicit a reaction.

"Remi," he says before pausing a moment then continuing on in a whisper, "I imagine taking you home to strip you down, kissing every inch of you. I fantasize about finding all those little spots to make you moan and sigh. I want to leave stubble burn on the insides of your thighs, marking you as mine. I'll tease you until you beg for more, and after you come, I'll hold you open while you scream for mercy without letting up."

Holy fuck, I'm wet just from hearing him talk like that.

Where the hell did that come from?

With that naughty mouth and the dirty talk coming out of it, it has me really wishing I wasn't on my period right now. I reach up and clamp my hand over his mouth to stop him from saying anything else.

"What the hell, Eli?" My breathing has gone choppy with the images he put in my head, and I'm hoping to avoid alerting the others around us to what was just going on. "Don't do that here!" I hiss.

He shoots me a smoldering look, and my eyes widen at just how unrepentant he is. I get the drift that nice polite Elliot is done waiting to take what he wants. I'm ready for this, I am. I keep reminding myself it's what I've been after.

Just not today.

Or tomorrow.

"I did say I wanted to take you home first," he points out. He's deliberately misunderstanding my protest. I glare at him now, or try to. Kind of hard to stay mad when I'm so turned on and not really mad, more frustrated with the timing. Our first time will be nice and *not* while I'm on my period.

"Fine, home first, no more talking like that 'til we're back. I'll fall off the bike." He mimes zipping his lips and locking them, and I roll my eyes at his antics. Guess that will just have to do.

We finish our ride and head back to the motorcycle, almost there when he stops.

"I forgot to throw these away, be right back." Eli holds up the cider cups as he backtracks to find a trashcan.

While he goes and takes care of that, I get my helmet on. He's back quickly, and we both get on the bike. I hold him tight with my head resting on his back as he pulls out of the lot.

I drift in thought on the ride home, enjoying the happiness flowing through me. I squeeze Eli a little tighter, and he briefly reaches to cover my hand with his own, warm and comforting.

Safe.

I haven't felt safe in a long, long time, and now I'm feeling it on the back of a motorcycle that should have brought up memories that put me in a funk, but instead, he's given me new ones to cherish. The motorcycle is a lot like another I was once on, where I also had that happy, safe feeling. I take it to mean I should let go of the past and enjoy my future.

Turning my thoughts to the guy I'm holding onto, my fingers itch to explore the abs that lay under them. With my hands tucked under his jacket, there's only the thin barrier of his t-shirt blocking me from his warm skin. I try to behave since I'm not sure if that would be too much of a distraction.

But I can't quite seem to help myself. I'm already plastered to him, chest to his back, making my breasts feel heavy, hips snug up to him where the vibrations can be felt in the seat reverberating through my thighs. Slowly, leaving ample time for him to stop me, one hand slips down to the hem of his shirt and my fingertips ease under the edge.

What's good for the goose… I feel him suck in a breath, and I can't tell if it's from my cold hands, my touch, or a combination of the two. I continue until I can trace the defined lines and ridges football training has given him. Just touching them makes my breath come faster, and I have to refrain from rubbing my chest on his back. I splay my fingers across his abdomen and rest then there for the rest of the ride before I cause a distraction that makes us wreck.

We pull up and into the garage after waiting for it to open. I dismount and take my helmet off. Eli has an intense look on his face as he turns to me. As soon as he's off the bike he roughly pulls me close, cupping my ass and tucking me tight to him, his groin and chest aligned with mine. With a look of arousal and pain on his face, he tilts his hips further into mine to grind them together. I let out a soft groan echoed by his. He just stares at me for what seems like minutes. Then he slowly leans down and barely brushes his lips against mine.

A whisper of a kiss, really.

Letting me go, he turns and begins unloading the saddle bags. He leaves the pumpkins on a shelf and takes a bag inside with him, telling me to hit the alarm on my way in.

What the fuck was that? Gets me all hot and he just walks away?

I wonder if he knows that I won't take it further right now. Or he's playing at a game that I don't know the rules to. If so, I think he might win with as worked up as I'm feeling right now. I have to admit it to myself— there's a little warm glow in my chest from the wonderful time I had.

I started out not wanting to care about him, but I don't think he or my heart is going to give me that choice.

Chapter Nine

The days pass by quickly. We've gotten into a bit of a routine, almost like a real couple, cooking, cleaning up, hanging out while watching movies or working on reading assignments companionably.

I'm not sure what to think of it all.

I know I have to talk to him soon, explain where I'm coming from. This situation won't last forever. I'll be going back to the dorms soon and after that to live with Alex. Eli has taken to snuggling while in the living area if we're just watching a movie and a kiss to the forehead when one or both of us go to bed. I feel like he's declared silent warfare on my reservations, and he's coming out the victor.

Randomly, it seems every time that I see him around the apartment, he's half-naked. Bedroom doors left cracked, so I can catch glimpses of all that skin. Lounging around in just shorts. Even when he's not working out he wears them around the apartment, tempting me. I've started using the gym myself, just to expel the frustration. Not that it's helping much. It's one of the two doors that access the fourth floor. I don't know what's in the other room, and when I asked, he said it was for the business.

I found the gym after seeing Eli coming downstairs, all sweaty and in those damn shorts, as I was coming up the stairs to the apartment.

And holy crow that was something to see.

Boy has some serious definition. I had to ball my hands into fists and cross my arms to keep from reaching out and touching as we passed by each other. Thinking I was avoiding his sweatiness, he scooped me up in a hug and rubbed his wet forehead in my neck as I squealed for him to stop. Little did he know that it totally gave me a legitimate excuse to cop a feel.

The day I decided that he had officially vowed to melt my brain with unrequited lust was the day I came home later than usual and heard the shower running. Hearing moaning as I walked down the hall to my room, I could see Eli's bedroom door was open as well as the bathroom door. Upon hearing the moan again, my heart plummeted into my stomach and my eyes started to burn.

First thought was he's screwing someone in there right now. How could he?! I stood there knowing I should leave but unable to move. Debating if I should confront them now or wait until they come out.

I wasn't going to be a coward. He couldn't do this to me; I wouldn't let him.

Tell me he wanted me, being patient and barely touching me, driving me crazy and then this? I'm beyond furious. I know his behavior is basically what I asked for, but I didn't ask him to fuck someone else after he chose to wait.

This was over, unacceptable.

And that's what really hurt, why I forced myself to push the door open. As I touched the door I heard another moan, this time with a name in it.

"Remi."

I could barely see through the fogged over glass of the shower, but what was going on was unmistakable. Forgetting that I was pissed a nanosecond ago, now I was rapt with attention on the show in the shower. My pulse was instantly through the roof, and lady town announced with fireworks that she's open for business.

Eli had one hand braced on the wall while the other was fisted around the length between his legs.

And holy cannoli, he was packing.

I'm going to have to plan for that.

Not that I was exactly sure what planning would entail to make that fit and while I had a few good ideas, that's what Google was made for.

Eli's hand was moving rapidly from base to tip, and his hips were pumping up to meet each downward stroke. His own hand didn't close all the way around his thickness. As he picked up the pace, he started panting between moans.

I knew as soon as I realized he wasn't with anyone else that I should have turned around and left, giving him his privacy. I'm not sure how I would feel if it had been the other way around.

Oddly, I found I was more turned on than off at the thought of Eli watching me the way I was watching him. As I continued to stare, Eli threw his head back and found his release. He straightened up from his slump against the wall, and I turned to go. I couldn't let him find me watching like a creeper.

Since then I've been walking around almost constantly with a lady boner. I've had my fair share of sexy thoughts, but this was getting ridiculous.

Maybe I'm turning into a guy.

That would explain the frequency. I am going to burn up. I don't think my heart rate is ever going to be back to normal, and I constantly feel flushed.

One evening while we are painting the little pumpkins that we had gotten from the festival, Eli asks if I'm feeling alright. I blush until I'm sure I resembled a tomato.

Eventually, I'll stop turning red around him, right? I feel like a ridiculous preteen pinking it up every five minutes.

"You've looked hot all afternoon, Remi. Do you have a fever?"

He reaches over to touch my forehead, smoothing away a few of the loose strands of hair that have come out of my messy bun. My breath hitches, and Eli smiles, an evil, knowing smile. "Are you having trouble with something, Remi? I could help with that, you know." His voice has dropped into a husky whisper as his fingers trail down my cheek, lower to my neck, then over the very edge of the swell of one breast. I hold my breath as I watch that hand, then he pulls back. "Say the word and I'll dive between those beautiful thighs in an instant." I almost choke on my own spit with his blunt remark.

His eyes stay locked onto my wide ones the entire time. I want to say yes; I want to beg him not to stop. But I don't, and he sees that hesitation. He swears, and after rinsing his brushes out he disappears into his room, shutting the door. Faintly, I hear the sound of the shower running.

I grin to myself; at least I'm not the only one in need of a cold shower.

Soon after, it's the day before the Halloween party, and Alex and I are in my room trying on the costumes we picked out earlier in the week.

"I can't believe you get to stay here; this place is awesome." I look around and agree with her. It *is* pretty fabulous here.

"Is Eli going to the party too?" Alex asks.

"I think so. A bunch of the other guys on the team are going to be there from what I've heard."

"So, what's going on with you and him? I'm guessing it's a little weird since he's been chasing after you since school started and now you end up living with him."

"It's actually been really nice. He said he doesn't feel right pushing a relationship with me while I'm staying here, so he's backed off until I say differently. He'll occasionally say things, or we'll talk or do stuff, but he stops the second I even remotely indicate I'm unsure. I'm not uncomfortable here if that's what you're getting at. "Actually," I say, trying to hide my embarrassed smile, "I kinda wish he'd stop being so tame. Dude is seriously making me frustrated."

"What happened? Tell me, tell me now!" Alex squeals, jumping up and down like a fangirl at a boy band concert.

"Really, Alex?" I say dryly, rolling my eyes at her antics that she knows annoy me. It's half the reason she does it. "I accidentally walked in on him showering…and I didn't exactly turn around and leave right away." Alex gives me raised eyebrows and an expectant expression.

"I want details. A shower encounter, unless you're naked too, isn't anything more than an oops. Spill." Alex is holding up a hairbrush like she's gonna whack me with it if I don't give her the gossip.

"Not a lot to tell. The shower door was frosted," I explain while giving her a look of disappointment, "but I could definitely tell *what* he was doing." I add on the last part with no small measure of glee.

"Shut the fuck up. You watched him do *that*? You perv!"

Alex reaches out and pushes my shoulder, but she doesn't exactly look scandalized. She seems more interested than anything else.

Do not punch best friend. I repeat, Do. Not. Punch. Friend. OMG… I'm jealous.

I don't think I've ever been jealous of my friend, and I shake it off. She wouldn't do that even if I made an engraved pass and gave it to her at this point. Girl code and all that stuff covered by it is sacred between us.

"I know, and I'm pretty sure he knows I was there too. He's been teasing me about being 'hot' since then. I thought he was in there screwing a girl, and I was pissed that he would say he wants me and then go bone someone else the first chance he had some privacy."

Even though the other female was just fictitious in my own head, I still get a little cranky thinking about it.

"So instead, you got an eyeful. You go girl. You should have just opened the door and climbed in. I'm sure he wouldn't mind." Alex waggles her eyebrows at me after her outrageous suggestion. I cover my eyes with my hand, cuz really, I was tempted and I know it.

"Alex," I groan.

"Fine. Alright so let's see it. Do the twirl." I spin around in my costume. "Shit, girl, that's hot and almost slutty even though you're covered. How did you pull that off? I can never get you in anything like this. Half the chicks there are going to have their ass cheeks hanging out. Including me," she says with a Cheshire grin.

I look down at my costume. A little face paint and some colored hair spray is all I'll need to finish off my Harley Quinn outfit. Technically, my ass cheeks *are* hanging out. They're just covered in these cute printed leggings I found that look like fishnets.

"What's Eli going as?"

"I'm not sure; he hasn't said. He's been really busy with football training and practice. From what he's said it sounds like they might get to the playoffs this year." I change into lounge clothes and put my costume up in the back of my closet so Eli doesn't see it if he comes in here.

Alex and I head out to the kitchen. I get two cups down and fill them with coffee and hand one to Alex, before setting out the cream and sugar, so we can both doctor our coffees. Eli comes in from practice along with a gust of air from the door bringing his scent with him. I inhale and sigh.

So, so good. Eli has taken to coming home directly from practice to shower here every chance he gets.

"I don't smell dinner," he says with a smile.

He knows I'm checking him out. Guess I am fairly obvious about it. I sigh again.

Alex turns to him with her mouth hanging open. She rapidly fixes that and blasts him with a glare.

"Excuse me? Did you just imply she should have dinner waiting on you?" Alex looks like she's ready to smack him.

"I was just teasing. Remi knows I appreciate her cooking, but she also knows she doesn't have to cook." He looks to me for help while Alex glares on.

I put my hands up.

"I'm not getting in the middle of this. It's too entertaining."

"So, ladies," Eli quickly throws out, "looks like I'm cooking dinner. Pizza or Chinese?"

"Good save, smart one." Alex looks slightly less murderous now. "I have to finish a paper for tomorrow, but you two have a good time." Alex winks and is out the door shortly after.

"Did you want to stay in and watch a movie or play a game? We can order delivery. My treat." Eli pauses his ordering, waiting on my reply.

"That sounds fantastic. Pizza? We can do half and half. Make mine mushroom, ham, and black olives, please. I'm going to straighten up my room some before I forget the mess. Alex brings new meaning to the name dervish. I've got clothes everywhere."

"Not a problem! I'll yell when it gets here."

Chapter Ten

We are eating gooey, cheesy pies thirty minutes later on the giant pillows.

"Movie or game?"

I don't really care either way, I am just comfortable sitting around.

"Whatever you like. I'm not particular." That's where I made my mistake.

"Twenty questions alright with you?" Eli looks nervous.

He's had this planned it seems.

"I suppose," I answer warily.

Where is he going with this?

"If you don't want to, that's okay. I just thought it would be a good way to get to know each other better."

"No, it's fine. Go ahead."

May as well get it all out there if we're going to be a couple. He'd probably find out eventually anyway.

"I'll start out easy. What's your full name?"

"Remington Reese Carter. My mom and dad's favorite things. Reese's cups were my mom's craving when she was pregnant with me, and of course Remington for my dad being in the military. What's yours?"

"Elliot Michael McAdams. My parents weren't as original as yours it seems. So, your dad is in the military?"

"Is that your question, or are you making conversation?" I would have rather avoided this question altogether, and now it's been brought up right away.

"That's my question."

"Technically he was in the military, and now he's in, or I guess was in the CIA. That's not something I usually spread around either for obvious reasons."

I don't want everyone knowing about my dad for personal and security reasons.

"I wouldn't say anything, Remi. Anything you tell me, if I even think you might be uncomfortable with it, I won't talk about around others." Eli looks so earnest as he says this that I believe him. "Your turn."

"When did you know you wanted to play football?"

I'm curious because he's told me before he's here on a scholarship for football and majoring in business, like me, and minoring in psychology.

"Forever, I think. I always liked to play it with my dad and brothers at home, and then when I was at the military academy, I joined the team they had. There weren't too many fun things to do there recreationally. That's actually how I met my roommates. They're a couple years older than me."

"You went to a military academy?"

I'm surprised by this and must have some weird expression on my face as Eli looks at me with a confused and inquiring expression. What are the odds of him answering with that?

Not many and I narrow my eyes in suspicion.

"Not your turn, pretty girl." He smirks at me. "It's mine." I wait impatiently for him to go on so I can get back to my questions. He looks like he's not sure he should ask his next one. He takes a deep breath and asks, "You said 'was' when you were talking about your dad. Did he pass away?"

Yep there it is. May as well get it over with.

"Technically, I'm not supposed to talk about it, but I trust you." I take a bolstering breath. "My dad disappeared on his last assignment when I was in high school. My mom and I don't know if he's alive or not. There was an investigation from his superiors, and we were questioned incessantly, but we don't know anything and they haven't found anything out either. Not that the investigators have shared anyway. It was my senior year. That's why I transferred here as a sophomore. I was supposed to be here with Alex as a freshman, but instead, I stayed home with my mom and took a gap year to help her out and did mostly online classes from home and a few at the local community college. Without a definitive answer on whether my dad took off on his own or something happened to him, all his accounts were frozen even though they were my mom's too. Not just my dad's. If he did take off, which I can't see him doing since he loves my mom and me, then they didn't want him to have access to resources. If he…"

I get choked up, and Eli sees it, pulling me between his open legs and turning me to rest mine over his thigh so he's cuddled around me.

"You don't have to continue on," he says, hugging me tighter and resting his cheek on my head. I feel him smelling my hair, and it's kind of sweet. I want to finish telling him, so I continue on.

"If he died, and they could prove it, they wouldn't have done anything. If he's missing or taken off, it's frozen until they find him or until they determine it's no longer needed as bait. If they released it to my mom, she could potentially give it to him if he contacted her. My college fund was in his name as well. My deposit had already been paid here, but there wasn't enough for a full year of school, so I made arrangements with special circumstance for the deposit to be held onto until I could transfer. I spent most of that first year picking up modeling jobs. I had done a couple ads when I was younger, but I needed something I could do to help mom out and still pay for school too. I got enough saved up between that year and the next while I was taking classes at the local community college, so I didn't get too far behind the others here. That's why Alex is a junior and I'm a sophomore. I didn't have enough credits to transfer in as a third year. I'll be twenty-one this May. I think that about covers it."

Eli doesn't say anything for a bit. When he does, he comes out with, "I don't just want to say I'm sorry. It doesn't seem adequate, but I'm not sure what else to say either. I hate that you had to go through that. Did they find anything at all?"

Even though it's not Eli's turn, I decide to answer his question. I think the game is essentially over anyway after everything I just told him.

"They found a motel room in an area he wouldn't have been in unless he had been assigned to it. The investigators wouldn't give us a lot of details. His luggage and some other things were left behind. As far as they can tell, since it wasn't there, the only thing he took was his identification. There wasn't any sign that he was taken against his will. They tracked his phone and vehicle GPS to find him and ended up there at that motel. The investigators asked us questions for months, but we didn't know anything other than he was supposed to be gone for a couple weeks on assignment. They check in every few months to see if he contacted either of us, and we were under surveillance for almost a year before they backed off. Even if my dad went rogue, I know he wouldn't contact us in any way; he would know they would be watching. And that's not something he would have done unless it was a survival situation. So that's it for the most part. I worked and then transferred and now here I am."

I chew on my lip, waiting for his response, and play with my necklace by dragging the charm around the chain.

"Maybe when the guys get back we can ask them to look into it. I only do work part-time because of football and full-time classes, but the others already graduated."

Eli's arm moves behind me, and his fingers begin playing with the ends of my hair as he speaks. I'm very aware of how I'm sitting in his lap and am unsure if I should move or not. I decide it's comfortable, so I stay where I am for now.

"What would your roommates be able to do to help? I'm not sure the agency would be willing to share any information. Besides that, I have enough money to pay for school and help my mom out, not enough to hire an investigative team." I don't want to seem ungrateful to Eli, but really, what can they do to help that hasn't already been done? As an afterthought I add, "I didn't know you worked here too. I just thought you were renting a room from them."

I turn enough to meet his gaze with the question.

"For one, if we helped, it would be because we wanted to, and two, I know the guys from the school we went to. After I graduated and had been offered a scholarship I met up with them here. One of the guys had this building left to him by some relative, an aunt I think." He looks down at me, staring at my hand that's still playing with the necklace. Swiftly changing the subject as if he knows I don't want to talk about my dad any longer, he asks, "What's that on your necklace? I don't think I've ever seen you without it."

I pull it outwards to show it to him. It's a silver disc with an R scripted on it.

"It's a locket that a couple friends gave to me years ago. I guess it was really a going away present since I only saw them once more after they gave it to me." I go to open it and show him the pictures inside. I figure now is as good a time as any to tell him about the guys, but right then my phone starts ringing. I go to answer it and see that it's Adam. "I should probably see what's up with him; it's pretty late for it to be a social call." I answer the phone to a slightly out of breath Adam. "Hello?"

"Remi? It's Adam. Hey, I lost my assignment for class and was wondering if you had it? I'm not too far from your building if you do and don't mind meeting me downstairs so I can copy it?"

Seems odd, but I don't see any reason to deny his request.

"Umm...yeah. Which class? I'm at home, so you can swing by, and I'll come down with it."

I don't want to invite him up, so I'm glad he suggested meeting downstairs.

"It's for the calculus class. I was sure I had written it down, but I can't find it in my notes at all. I'll be there in a few minutes."

I hang up and grab the assignment, pulling on a jacket and slippers as I head for the door.

I tell Eli I'm running some school work to Adam downstairs as I see him cleaning up the living room. I happily see that our conversation is over as well. Eli tells me to use the copier in the den area, so I use the multipurpose printer/scanner then get out to the sidewalk to wait on Adam.

As I'm standing there, I get a text message, but before I can check it, Adam walks up. "I copied the notes for the assignment. Hope you have enough time to get it done before class tomorrow." I hand him the copied pages from my notebook.

"Thanks, Remi. I owe you one." He takes the papers I hold out. He stands there for a minute, seeming to want to say more. "So, I'm going to the big costume party tomorrow night at the beta frat. Would you like to go with me?"

Now I'm wondering just how 'lost' his homework had actually been.

"Actually, I'm going with Alex, but if you're going too, I'm sure we'll see you there," I answer noncommittally with a smile to take the sting out of the rejection.

"Oh, okay. Well, I'll be looking for you."

He seems disappointed. I'm going to need to think of a polite way to tell him I'm not interested in him like that soon, before this crush he has going on gets any worse.

"See you tomorrow, Adam," I say as he walks away. He waves back and disappears around the corner.

I turn to go back inside and almost scream, instantly swinging out at my attacker. My fist connects with Eli's arm he puts up to block the blow. He comes the rest of the way out of the doorway and grabs my shoulders to steady me. I struggle to catch my breath and slow my heart rate. It had spiked fast enough to make me dizzy. "Holy crap, dude, you scared me." Now that I'm over my scare, I laugh a little.

"Sorry, I just wanted to make sure you were alright and lock up for the night." He looks like he wants to say something else too but pauses before teasing me. "Didn't think you were going to hit me for it though." I feel silly for overreacting and apologize.

"I'm sorry, you startled me, and I didn't realize it was you. I thought I was alone out here. I'm gonna head up to bed, see you tomorrow?" He nods his head, and I go back upstairs.

As I'm getting into bed, I plug my phone in and see the message icon still showing in my notification bar. It's from an unknown number.

I know where your father is.

That's it. Nothing else, no number to contact back. If this is a prank, it pisses me off. I put the phone down and go brush my teeth and wash my face. I'll call the investigative team tomorrow and let them know about the message; it's the first thing I've heard about my father since he disappeared. I find it a little odd too that I was just talking about him to Eli before I got the message.

I try to put it out of mind and get some rest.

Elliot

While Remi was downstairs, I snuck into her room. I want to surprise her with my costume tomorrow, but I don't know what she's wearing. She's left something hanging over on the desk chair, and when I get to it, I see that's it the costume. Getting what I came for, I turn to leave when I notice my coin that all the students get from the academy I went to. I frown, wondering how it ended up in here. It had been in a drawer in my room. I grab it and take it with me, setting it on my dresser before I make my way around the building to check the doors for the night. Deciding to check on Remi too as she hasn't come back yet, I go out the door she's outside of.

I get one heck of a surprise too. Glad to know she can defend herself if it comes to it. If it weren't for my own training for work. I'd probably have a bruised face.

My mind drifts back to my plans for tomorrow. I'm excited and hope to pull off the idea I had. If things go well, the wait will finally be over, and Remi will finally, officially be mine. I can't wait.

Chapter Eleven

Remington

I wake up to a knock on my bedroom door. "Remi? You up yet? There are some people here to see you." I open my eyes. It's barely light out, can't even be seven yet.

Who the heck is coming to see me at the ass crack of dawn?

"I'm awake. Be right there," I call out in reply.

Throwing back the covers and swinging my legs over the side of the bed, I grab a hoodie and throw it on over my tank and shorts then pull on the fuschia fuzzy socks I left out last night. After brushing my teeth and hair I head out to meet my visitors.

As I get to the kitchen, I see Agents Bricker and Norman sitting at the breakfast bar. Eli turns with coffees for them both and goes to get another for me. He's barefoot and in sweats and a tank with an open zip up thrown over it. His blond hair is still mussed from sleep, and he looks hot and adorable all at once. I reluctantly drag my attention away from him to address the two visitors who obviously notice the interaction.

I don't give a shit, and they can go fuck themselves.

"Umm…someone want to tell me why you're in my kitchen?"

I glare at them both, crossing my arms over my chest while realizing the slip of saying *my* kitchen, but since Eli doesn't contradict me, I go with it.

Eli looks at me in surprise, probably at my tone and attitude, and comes over to stand next to and slightly behind me. Being supportive while allowing me to handle it. I shoot him a grateful look. I didn't expect that out of him. I expected him to make himself scarce or be aggressive.

"We're here because-- actually if you could excuse us, Mr. McAdams, we'd like to speak to Miss Carter alone." Agent Norman looks annoyed when Eli doesn't immediately acquiesce to his almost politely veiled demand.

Eli looks down at me for an affirmative. He'll leave if I ask him, I know that, but I don't want him to.

"Eli can stay; he knows about my dad."

Agent Norman instantly looks thunderous while his partner Bricker opens her mouth to say, "That is highly inappropriate for him to know about an agency investigation. Who gave you leave to discuss it?"

I cannot stand that woman. She's half the reason my life was shit after my dad disappeared. She's rude and crass and thinks she's better than everyone else.

"I don't need permission to talk about my dad. You have stalked my mom and me for almost three years. We don't know what happened, and I'm not putting up with your attitude, so can it or get the fuck out."

I'm furious and want to smack someone. I realize I'm holding Eli's hand and squeezing the snot out of it in my anger. I make an effort to loosen my hold without letting him go. I'm not sure if he reached for me or I reached for him, but I'm glad for it either way.

Snarkily, Agent Bricker continues on, "You are to inform the agency of your residence at all times, as well as all phone numbers and email you can be contacted at. You must notify the agency of any communication you receive that could potentially be from Agent Carter. Care to guess what we found when we showed up at your dorm this morning?" She doesn't wait for me to answer. "We found a construction crew arriving and were told that the students had been relocated…several weeks ago. We had to track your phone to get your location as the administrative buildings aren't open for business for the day yet. All that after the fact that you didn't report the communication you received pertaining to your father when it came in. At this point, I think you may need to come in for another interview. Go dress and meet us outside."

As she turns to leave, obviously expecting I'll follow orders, I lose my temper.

"Excuse the hell out of you. You have no right to come here. I don't answer to you. My whereabouts or residence are also not your business. And *what the fuck* do you mean by saying I didn't report a communication. Do you have my phone bugged?"

I'm stepping forward with every question and end the last on a growl. Now I'm directly in Bricker's face with Norman watching Eli closely.

Bricker smirks, and I want to plant my fist in that smug face. I feel Eli's arm circle my waist and pull me back into his chest. "You received a communication last night stating that someone knows where your father is. You didn't report it. That leads us to believe that you know something as well or soon will. We have no intention of being left out of the loop any further."

"I opened that message as I was going to bed last night and figured I would call it in when I got up. Obviously, you woke me up. I haven't even had a chance to report it, and you're here, up my ass, trying to drag me in for an interview. Guess what, lady? I'm not going to any interview; I'm not talking to you, period. Contact my attorney if you would like to speak to me, and you'll have to arrest me to get me to go with you. As I haven't exactly done anything other than take the temporary housing the university arranged after my dorm flooded, and I didn't try to contact the agency at almost midnight last night, I think I will be safe in saying get the fuck out. This is harassment, and my attorney will be filing a grievance against you directly. Norman, I know you just follow Bricker around as your head is too far up her ass to do anything for yourself. If that changes, let me know. As far as I'm concerned, you're both done here, and Bricker, that's permanently for you."

I've walked to the door as I've been talking, and stand with it wide open, waiting on them to leave. I follow them out and go downstairs to make sure the doors lock behind them and as soon as they're gone, grip the sides of my head and let out a frustrated shriek.

I need an outlet before I chase her down and do something to get arrested. I am so sick of this shit following me around and fucking with my life. I'm also worried about Eli's reaction now that it's invaded his home.

As if thinking about him conjures him up, he comes running down the hall. He's sporting a worried expression until he sees me then he starts laughing. I scowl at him.

"Oh my god, Remi. I thought you were going to punch her. I'm sorry! If I would have known what they were up to, I wouldn't have let them in. I'm going to do a full scan of the building in case they left any monitoring devices, then I'll take care of your phone and check your car too just to be safe. Don't worry, I won't let them spy on you anymore. Or me. If I'd known sooner, I would have already taken care of it. I should have at least checked though and would have if the boarder we had gotten was anyone else. The guys would kill me if I let us get spied on again."

Without showing a hint of outward care, he breezily walks back upstairs to get to the fourth floor. I shake my head at his back in a little bit of disbelief that he didn't freak out over all that. I head back in and go take a shower to calm down and get dressed for the day.

When I come back out, Eli has a little pile of plastic and metal pieces in a glass of water.

"I got these off your car and from everywhere they were while they were in here. That's a little overkill in my opinion, and if they don't have a warrant for it, our legal team is going to make their lives mighty uncomfortable." Holding out his hand, he gestures toward my pocket. "Here, let me see your phone." I pull it out and hand it over. Before I can protest, he pulls the SIM card out of it, breaks it in half, and tosses the pieces into the water with the other broken bits. He picks out a new card from a little case and pops it in the slot before powering it back up. "Should be fine now. Just don't let anyone near it. If you even think anyone has too much interest in it, let me know, and I'll check it again." With that, he stands up and collects his gear and the glass of water. "I gotta get ready for school." I hurry to speak before he leaves the room.

"Thank you, Eli. I should have known we were still being watched, my mom and me, I mean. I shouldn't have brought this here to you; I wasn't thinking."

I feel a little ashamed at not telling him about the possibility and avoid meeting his eyes. He's been nice about it, but would I have been okay with it if the situation were reversed? I can't say for sure.

"Not a problem, Remi. I told you I work for the security team here too. If I can't handle a few bugs, I'm in the wrong business." He leans over, reaching out and tilting my face up to meet his eyes. He plants a kiss on my forehead, before releasing me to go to his room. "I'm going to get ready. I have class and a game to prepare for."

While he seemed reassuring, I still have a niggle of doubt that he's alright with everything.

He walks out without looking back while I stand and stare after him.

Chapter Twelve

I hurry home from my last class and have a can of soup for dinner since Eli sent me a text earlier saying he would be out when I got in. After showering as quickly and thoroughly as I can, I put my bag together with my costume and sundries in it. I was going to get ready with Alex at her place.

After showering I put on some black leggings, a lacy plum colored cami top, and a charcoal cable knit sweater that hits me mid-thigh. With some slouch boots and a scarf I'm almost ready to go, finishing by pulling my hair up and putting on some mascara. It isn't getting too cold out yet and with all the lights and other people in the stadium, it should stay warm enough, so I only grab a light jacket on the way out just in case.

When I get to the stadium, I park on the outer edge of the designated lot to hopefully not get stuck in the traffic jam that usually ensues at the end of sporting events at this college. I find Alex waiting near the entrance. The attendant scans our student IDs and the stamp that lets us into events, and we head into the venue.

We stop by concessions to grab drinks and nachos and some other snacks to hold us over during the game. As we make our way to our seats I tell Alex about my morning visitors. To say she is outraged is an understatement. I think she may actually be angrier than I was and has several inventive things that Bricker could do involving her head and rear end.

I laugh so hard at her descriptions that I get a few strange looks from other people. Hearing Alex so outrageously defend me cheers me up immensely.

"I cannot believe the audacity of that woman. Have you and your mom not cooperated enough yet? You postponed college, for fuck's sake, over the crap they pulled with your savings. Even though you contributed part of that money yourself. They're only doing this in the hopes that your father is monitoring you and sees what they're doing and tries to help so they can catch him. What they don't realize is your father loves you and your mom. He wouldn't just take off on you both unless he had no choice or was taken by force."

Alex's cheeks are flushed from her ire and subsequent rant. I know she's right, but it still upsets me though that my mom and I are being treated like criminals. As I think of Bricker some of my anger flares back up. I'll figure out a way to make that woman's life hell one way or another after the crap this morning.

We make it to our seats in the stands, and I fess up about being worried about Eli. I only just told him about everything last night, and then he was immediately bombarded with it this morning.

Alex rolls her eyes at me. "Remi, the dude is nuts about you. You have absolutely no reason to worry about that."

I consider her words and decide to wait and see what he has to say. We're sitting fairly close to where the team benches are, and I'm hoping Eli will hear us cheering for him or at least see us more easily if he happens to look. He's really grown on me so much the last few weeks. I was surprised he didn't try to take advantage of my proximity while I've been staying with him.

I finger my necklace, thinking of one person who would have taken what he wanted, not that I would have minded. Alex notices what I'm doing.

"Still missing them, huh?"

Alex mimes zipping her lips when I shoot her a look. We've had this discussion many times, but it doesn't change anything and never will. One day we'll both accept that.

Turning back to the field, I see the pep squad is riling up the crowd. The team is getting ready to come out. The stomping and the chants start, and you can feel the energy in the air from the excitement. Football is a major draw for the university; people from all over come to the games. A cheer goes up as the players start to run out. They jog out and do their warm up, some of the guys posing for the journalists and media majors. Finishing up with the routine, they line up and return to their area right below us. The other team is coming out next. They don't get quite the reception, but as they're a close school and major rival they have a decent amount of support here tonight. Locating Eli's number, I see him huddled with a group of players around a coach.

"What position does Eli play?" I ask Alex.

She turns to me with an incredulous look on her face. It mirrors a couple others sitting around us as they overhear my question. *Yeah, I should probably know that,* I think with a wince and a shrug.

"Oh my god, Remi, how do you not know that? You live with the guy!"

Yep, thanks for that, Alex. I look around, hoping she wasn't overheard, and of course, no such luck. Now a good majority of the girls within earshot have turned slightly murderous or at least maiming looks my way. I feel I may need some body armor to get out of here intact. I kick Alex, and when she notices a few of the looks as well, she gets a devious smile on her face. "He's a wide receiver. A very good one at that. He'll probably get drafted. But I can see how you might have been too busy with your own receiving to bother remembering that." Alex is now openly laughing.

I'm gonna kill her. Dead. Very, very dead.

"Alex, shut up. I cannot believe you just said that," I hiss to her, beyond mortified. "You know very well I'm not sleeping with him. What are you doing?" My best friend has a serious lack of boundaries, but she's usually not this terrible.

"Staking your claim for you since you won't," she whispers back, completely unrepentant. I give up.

"Just watch the game! It's starting."

Right about then Eli's group breaks up, and he looks up at the stands, quickly finding me and blows me a kiss. My mortification tries to return with a vengeance; I think I might be in trouble with him and Alex ganging up on me tonight. Between the two of them I don't stand a chance. I decide just to go with it. Not like I don't want his attention. I give a big smile and wave, unable to bring myself to blow a kiss back.

The game starts, and our school's team immediately gets the ball. The first half passes quickly with Eli catching the ball multiple times, and he even scores two of the touchdowns. At halftime, Alex and I go to the bathroom and wait in line with the dozen other like-minded students. As we finally get into stalls I hear other girls start a conversation at the sink.

"Did you hear Elliot McAdams has a girlfriend? And she's not even on the pep squad. I can't imagine Brittany is going to take kindly to that. She's had a thing for him for the last two years. Even I thought she was getting somewhere when I saw them talking in the parking lot after practice the other night."

The sound of the hand dryers cut out whatever is said next, and by the time it's off and I come out the girls are gone. My chest hurts, and my throat feels heavy. If what those girls said is true, I need to put a stop to what is going on between us. I don't want to jump to conclusions, and I can't exactly ask Eli at the moment, but I'm pissed all the same.

"They're just jealous, you know. I'm sure they knew you were in here; they probably saw you in line," Alex consoles me as soon as I come out, verifying she overheard as well. She rubs my shoulder, and we head out back to our seats. "Don't let them see they bothered you. I don't think Eli would do that and especially with Brittany. He was probably trying to scrape the nasty off if she touched him. She's been with half the team, and that's not an exaggeration. Not that that would be a problem, but it's only because she wants to be popular. One of her teammates is best friends with my roommate, and I overheard them talking about her looking to land anyone with enough talent to go pro. She's barely keeping her grades good enough to stay on the squad."

I feel a little better, but I still wonder. We watch the last part of the game. Eli gets hit right as he catches a pass. He quickly gets up and shows that he still has the ball.

The crowd is going wild.

With a few minutes left in the game, he's almost close enough to score again. The final result is in favor of Easton 52-38, and Alex and I head out to the parking lot with the rest of the crowd to our cars. Alex is parked somewhat close to me, so we make our way to our vehicles and go to her place to get ready for the party. Normally, I would have gone to wait on Eli and congratulate him, but I'm a little nervous to see him and I want to get started on my costume.

After we're both finally ready and have drunk half a bottle of wine each, we walk to the party. It's only a few blocks away as Alex's apartment is close to that side of the campus. We carry our disposable travel coffee cups with lids, the remainder of the wine divided between them. I'm not drinking anything without opening it myself tonight. Definitely learned my lesson last time.

When we get to the house the music is loud, there are decorations everywhere, and the costumes are a mix of classic and outlandish. Everything from a werewolf to a guy dressed as jailbird Paris Hilton in a blond wig, big square sunglasses, and an orange jumpsuit with sparkly pink high heels.

I think that one may be my favorite of the night.

The guy stuffed a neon pink bra, and his chest hair was poking out of the partially unbuttoned top. As I laugh I snort a little, causing Alex to roll her eyes at me. Alex and I make our way over to a group of people she knows that are beckoning to her. I really need to be more social. I have no idea who the majority of the partiers are.

As I'm standing there, an arm curls around my waist and a mouth with points in it latches onto my neck.

"Well, hello there, pretty girl," is whispered in my ear. After I throw an elbow into the body behind me, I get released. When I turn around I see it's a sparkling, fanged vampire, complete with red contacts. "Sorry, Remi, couldn't resist." It takes a minute, but I realize it's Adam. I smile at him so he knows I'm not upset. I see he's noticed my outfit now. "Hot damn, Remi, that is one insanely sexy costume. Did you pick it for me? Please say it was for me. Please, please!" Now Adam is fangirling it up, trying to get a laugh. He's such a goof.

"Keep it up, Adam, and I'm going to question what your actual gender is," I say with a straight face. That is until he immediately stops jumping and his face blanks, then I bust up laughing, catching the attention of the group Alex had stopped to talk to.

"She's got your number, Trent!" another guy from the group yells.

"Trent?" I question Adam.

"My last name. Geez girl, just how oblivious are you to me? I'm wounded." He puts a hand to his chest and one to his forehead, acting like he's going into a swoon. I turn pink in embarrassment.

"I'm sorry, Adam. I was just thinking I need to be more social; I don't really know anyone here besides you and Alex."

As I was talking to Adam a girl with a black pixie cut, dressed as a cat, pushes her way between me and Adam. I take in the leather bustier, fishnets, and stilettos.

"Remi, right?" she says.

She points her finger at me with the other hand on her hip. If I were to take a guess from the attitude and the girls around her that I recognize from the dance squad, I'd have to say this is Brittany. What luck. I see that her entourage behind her are all dressed similarly, each done up as different animals. I see a bunny, a cat in a calico outfit, a fox, and I'm not sure what the last girl is supposed to be. Maybe a skunk or a raccoon. *Poor choice of costume.*

"Yes, can I help you?" I ask as I arch an eyebrow.

Too bad I didn't complete my Harley Quinn costume with the bat and a wad of bubble gum. If I had known I was going to star in my own mean girls scene, I could have used something to prop on my shoulder and pop in my mouth while standing there and looking badass right about now. So glad I didn't wear the fishnet leggings even if they *were* opaque and went with some two-toned pink and blue tights that were slightly sheer instead.

"I just wanted to let you know that I'm going out with Eli. I heard you thought you were dating and told some girls in the bathroom at the game. Before you made a fool of yourself, I thought I'd let you know I've been with him every night this week."

She's obviously looking for a reaction or a capitulation. Unfortunately for her, that's not something she's going to get.

I stand there for a few long seconds, trying to get my mirth under control so that I don't laugh in her face. I don't see how that would help the situation, and I also don't really feel like getting into a fight over a guy.

I hear Alex snort behind me and say, "Now *that's* catty."

And…I totally lose it. Bent over laughing 'til tears come down, I rub at them, forgetting my makeup. Well, shouldn't matter too much. Harley isn't really known for being put together. As I'm pulling my composure back together, I see a guy coming towards me with his arms open.

"Toots, cupcake, darlin'..." the voice booms out, garnering more attention.

"No. Freaking. *Way*!"

This from Alex and Adam simultaneously. I feel the urge to reciprocate, cuz I'm pretty sure I know who this white-faced, tattooed killer is. Throwing caution on its ass, I span my arms wide and launch myself at him with my own declaration.

"Puddin'!"

The Joker catches me mid air and swings my legs around his waist before dipping me and laying the hottest kiss ever square on my mouth. Tongue and teeth with a full ass grab. His hands so completely engulf my cheeks that his fingertips are touching the sensitive place in the bend of my thighs. Millimeters from being pornographic in this crowd. With a giggle, I tap his shoulders, and he lifts me upright.

"Now our costumes are complete. Had to smear the lipstick on the both of us, you know?" His face is so close to mine that I can see his familiar green eyes and the greasepaint in his hair turning it dark and green.

He continues to hold me as he turns to the group of girls behind me. Totally ignoring the rabid animals, because that really just sums up the vibe coming off those girls, he greets Alex and Adam.

"So, Eli," I start out all innocence and curiosity. "Brittany here tells me you're dating, and she's been shagging you every night this week at your place. Should I be worried about where my lips just were?" I ask Eli this with a devilish grin on my face, but Brittany and crew can't see my face from this angle.

I know she wasn't at the apartment, but she must not know that I'm staying there. I've not exactly broadcast the news, and I don't think anyone else that knows has either. I get my facial expression under control and give Eli a proper scowl.

"I would try to put this nicely and do it in private, but I don't imagine that would get my message across clearly. Brittany, I think you may have me confused with another team member. I know you like to jump from bed to bed to find your future meal ticket, but mine hasn't been one of them. The only other bedroom I've been in besides my own, alone, mind you, is Remi's here. I heard costumes being discussed last night and waited until she was asleep to peek in her closet so I could match. If that doesn't spell it out enough for you, ask one of your friends. I can tell they understand."

I hear Adam making sizzling noises next to me. I start laughing again. He adds his own commentary, "Just to be clear, that means Eli isn't interested in your nasty ass. Most of us aren't, by the way, just in case you were wondering. We seem to have better taste." He imparts this with a quick wink to me. I just smile and shrug. What else can I do?

I unhook my legs from around Eli's waist and start to slide them down. I can feel his arms tense as he doesn't seem to want to let go, but we're causing a scene I would rather avoid.

"Let's go get a drink," I say when my feet hit the ground. As we turn to go, I ask Alex and Adam if they would like anything. We get to the kitchen area, and I head for the tubs of ice with closed drinks. I pull out several and make sure the seals are intact.

"Looking for drugs, Remi? I don't think the bottles are spiked or the kegs. The mixed drinks are another matter." I turn and see Christian leaning against the wall.

"So, you knew they were spiked at the last party? You're a dick." I walk past him without looking at him and return to Alex. As I hand her and Adam their drinks, I realize I've lost Eli. I see a small crowd gathering around the kitchen. Crap, that's not good. I make a beeline for the kitchen and have to push my way through. An arm tries to reach around me to pull me back, but I twist out to the side and slip through. Eli has Christian by the throat against the wall. I can't hear what he's saying, but it must be bad as Christian is red-faced and holding his hands up in surrender. I reach out and put my hand on Eli's bicep.

"Hey, leave him be. He's not worth getting into trouble. We'll tell the guys that live here about the drinks, and they can take care of it from there." Eli looks at me for a moment then finally releases Christian who slides down the wall a ways, coughing. With a nasty look promising retribution, he takes off into the crowd.

"Anyone know where Brandon is?" Eli asks. "The open drinks are spiked with who knows what this time. They need to be dumped out."

A few minutes later, a guy comes into the kitchen from another entrance and comes up to Eli. I realize this must be Brandon. He's older than most of the people here. He talks to Eli briefly, looks at me, and then gestures to a few other guys that head for the drinks. They start inspecting everything, making sure the seals are intact or throwing it out if it's been broken. I hear Brandon tell Eli thanks, and we head back to my friends.

"Remi, I can't take you anywhere, woman. You seem to be a trouble magnet." I turn to Alex, outraged, only to see that she's teasing me. "Let's go dance! I have a feeling you're going to get kidnapped eventually."

"I want a dance too, sugar plum, don't forget me." This from Adam. I give a grimace at the 'sugar plum.' "Hey," he protests, jerking a thumb to indicate Eli, "he doesn't get to be the only one giving you endearments. I think sugar actually suits you. I love sweet things." His voice drops as he leans in. "I'd love to find out exactly how sweet that is. Don't forget about me, Remi."

With that, he steps a few feet away to talk to others. I see him glancing back and forth and feel flushed. He's not taking his eyes off me for long. Whether or not I consider him as just a friend, that was hot. Undeniably hot. I can see Alex giving me her devilish look and shake my head. I don't need a fight; I'm just here to have fun. Eli looks perturbed, but he loses the look as I hook my arm through his.

"Remi, I don't believe we've ever danced together." I grin and motion to indicate that we have not.

He leads me into the next room where the music is louder and the floor has been cleared to make a large dance floor. There's already quite a few people out dancing on it. The song has a medium-paced tempo going on, and I slide effortlessly into Eli's embrace. He holds one of my hands and puts the other on my hip. I put my free hand on his shoulder. He starts moving hips in a smooth rocking motion as he steps forward, guiding me around a small area. *Holy hip wiggles, batgirl, he's good at this!* The surprise must show on my face. "Bet you thought I couldn't dance, just so you know. I have every intention of having that begging happening tonight." I swallow hard. Eli is doing something with the rhythm that brings first our hips then chests into contact. All I can do is follow. Butterflies are starting to rise up in my stomach. He's so hard all over. Football training is rigorous, and it shows. Even through his clothes you can see the muscle definition. Everywhere we touch, I feel the ridges on me. He's so much larger than me, and everything combined is really turning me on. I lick my lips, and I see his gaze dart down to them and stay there. Suddenly, the pace of the song picks up and so do his moves. I'm dipped and twirled until I'm breathless. I realize we've gathered an audience.

I've been so in my own world with Eli that I didn't even notice. As I come back up, pulled in close from a dip, I dart my tongue out and swipe at the hollow of his neck, tasting his slightly salty skin. I feel his inhalation of breath, and he grinds our hips together briefly, making me gasp in turn. This is going to turn inappropriate shortly if it keeps up. Right then I feel a hand tap my shoulder. It's Adam.

"May I cut in? I think someone needs some cool down time unless you want a video of one of our star players getting it on in the middle of a party. The coaches don't care about what goes on behind closed doors, but I think they might frown upon something like that getting around." Eli reluctantly lets go of my hand after surreptitiously looking around at the attention. After he moves into the area without dancers, Adam speaks. "I never really had a chance, did I?" He sounds sad. I look up at him.

"Adam, I'm sorry. I didn't try to pursue anything with anyone. It's just sort of happened. I do like you. You've been so nice to me. Not that you're just nice, I know guys hate that term. You're extremely attractive, but I have feelings, serious ones, for Eli. Maybe if I hadn't met him.

I've been trying not to get into a relationship, but again, it sort of just happened anyway." I hold his stare; he's hurt I can tell. He really has been great though. "Please don't take your friendship away from me. I don't have many friends, and I don't want to lose this one." I lean in and hug him. The song has switched to an actual slow one, and we sway to it. He holds on tightly for a moment then pulls back.

"I might have to take some time, but I won't leave you. I like you too much. If he messes with you though, I'm going to kick his ass, star football player or not, and I'm still calling you sugar plum!" With that, Adam smiles and spins me out. We dance to a few more songs before Alex joins us. Eventually, we're all hot and sweaty. I think my makeup is beginning to run and excuse myself from the dancing.

"Alex, I need a drink, as in water, and I think I'm ready to head home." I pull my phone out of my pocket and see that it's after one in the morning. "That would explain why I'm tired. You care if I head out? I'm sure Adam would make sure you make it home." Adam nods his head in the affirmative. Eli appears like he was summoned; he must have still been watching me.

"Ready to go, toots?"

"Is that name going to stick? If so, I'm calling you puddin'." I laugh and poke him in the chest, doing more damage to my poor finger than his hard pecs.

"Yes, I'm pretty sure it is. I want a daily reminder of the first time you publicly claimed me." He smiles devilishly at me. It really suits him, that naughty look.

I realize with a start that yes, I did claim him. In front of everyone. He continues, "It's about time if you ask me. I've been chasing you for over two months. Good thing I don't give up easily." He leans down to nuzzle my neck. "Let's go home. I want you. Badly." He presses his front to my hip, and I can feel exactly how much he wants me.

"Yes, I do think we're having the same thoughts," I say, not even pretending to not understand.

We start walking as it's not that far from campus and the night isn't terribly cold. We go most of the way in silence and make it into the hallway of our building where he starts kissing me. He lets up for a moment to swing me up into his arms and take the steps two at a time, getting us into the apartment while barely letting up for air. He drops us down on one of the large sofas. Our hands are all over each other. His tongue is moving to the same rhythm against mine as his hips are nestled against the juncture between my legs. I feel my blood thumping low in my body. I want him so much, and I know I'm already wet.

He pulls back just enough to speak. "Are you sure?" With my affirmative nod, he pulls us both up and continues to his room. "Let's shower first. Actually, you shower first in here, and I'll go to the hall shower. I don't think I'll wait if we're in there together, and I want it to be special. Not hurried against a wall." I'd be down with a wall. Maybe later.

I feel my heart melt. He's such a great guy. I lean in to give him a simple sweet kiss. Just a brush of lips against each other. "Eli-", "Remi-" We both go to speak at the same time. "You go first."

"Remi, I think- No, I know, I'm in---" I put my hand over his mouth. I know where this is going, and I definitely need to be showered first, because if he says what I think he's going to, I'm not waiting to jump his bones. "Go shower. I'll be right back."

I head for my bathroom and strip, turning on the water to warm up. I quickly wash my body of the sweat from dancing, but it takes three shampoos before my hair stops running colors. I get out and towel off, brush my hair, and throw on a long tank top, fuzzy socks (bright orange this time) and some undies. With a deep breath, I make for Eli's room.

Chapter Thirteen

He's already showered and is bare in his bed other than a pair of boxers that hug him while showing him off everywhere. I take him in, excited I'm finally going to touch all that. Every bit of it. I'm claiming him as my own. I take another deep breath. I know I have one more thing to do before this happens.

"You look nervous. We don't have to do this if you don't want to, you know?" There's no anger, just concern that I might not be ready for this step in our relationship even though I was obviously so ready earlier.

I take another breath. "It's not that. I just want to be clear before we go any further. This means me and you. Period. I'm not into casual dating."

There, that's plain enough.

"Agreed. You're it for me, Remi. I love you." I freeze, knowing he's waiting on me to reciprocate his declaration. I do, but I've been in love before. Am still in love from before.

"I-," I'm not sure how to say it.

"You don't have to say it back. I just wanted you to know how I feel. It's okay if you don't feel it yet." He's so freaking patient and understanding. How the heck am I going to tell him?

"I do, Eli. I do love you. I just… also love someone else," I say in almost a whisper. I dare to look up from my hands that I've squeezed together so hard that they're white around the edges.

Eli sits up. "What do you mean, you love someone else? Are you cheating on someone with me, Remi? Because from what you just said a minute ago I can't believe you'd do that. I feel the same way; I don't share." For the first time tonight I hear anger in his voice.

Anger that I would cheat on someone and him too essentially.

"I'm not with anyone else, Eli. It's not exactly like that." I see him visibly relax, but he's still wary.

"Explain it then, because what I'm imagining isn't good in any way right now." Some of the anger is back.

"It's a really long story. The short explanation is that I've thought I'd been in love more than once, but due to the situations at the time we weren't able to stay together. Frankly, Eli, my life has been kinda screwed up for a while. That's why I didn't want to get close to you." I want to reach out and touch him, but I need to let him decide what he wants now, without any type of coercion from me. I just hope he chooses me. I can't say I would do the same if roles were reversed.

"More than one? So, you're in love with multiple men? How does that happen?"

"Hey now, it could be women!" He just gives me a dry look. So maybe I'm trying to deflect this conversation. Really, who wouldn't in my shoes? "I don't know that I'm still in love with them. Or even that it actually was more than really caring about them. It felt a lot like I do about you right now though. I'm only bringing this up *because* of the fact that there were strong feelings, and that I was never able to have any kind of closure when we were separated. Feelings don't just go away for no reason, Eli. I was trying to be honest. I'm not explaining this right." I rub my face in frustration.

I should have just kept my mouth shut. As if he can sense what I was thinking, Eli replies.

"I'm glad you told me. It doesn't change how I feel about you. I'm upset about it, but I think anyone would be, really." He reaches out and grabs my hand and we stare at each other for a few moments. I blow out a breath, and my pale hair flutters up with it, partially dry now.

One more thing. I get up the courage to spit it out.

"There's more. I'm-" Eli raises his eyebrows, waiting.

"More what? You still see them? You have a secret love child? A closet drinker? What else could there be after that?" Eli's words are light, but his tone is frustrated.

"No, I don't see them. Haven't spoken to any of them in years. It's that, umm, I've not actually…well…had sex."

The last part is fast and quiet. I'm looking down, blushing badly now. What twenty year old is actually still a virgin anymore? Well, maybe not technically a virgin, just not actual intercourse. And it certainly wasn't for lack of trying.

"Did I hear that right? Are you telling me you're a virgin?" If his eyebrows go any higher, they're going to crawl off his head.

I scowl at him and snap.

"It's not like I tried to keep it that way. I'm very good at getting interrupted, and then all that stuff happened with my dad. I didn't really have time or the inclination for a boyfriend, and I didn't just want to do it with the first guy I came across. I would at least want to be in like with him, if not love." I'm annoyed now. It's definitely a joke with Alex, and I don't run around advertising it. I mean, really, who tries to lose it twice and doesn't? Maybe third time's the charm? Although with the way this is shaping up, it really might not be. I groan and bury my face in my hands. "This is so, so not how I imagined this going. *Again*. What is wrong with me?"

"There's nothing wrong with you, Remi. I was just surprised. And now I feel a bit like an ass. I can't just jump you now. It should be special. Come here." He pulls me down so we're cuddling.

"What if I told you I didn't want anything special?" I turn to face him and put my hand on his cheek. Looking into his eyes. "What if I just want to do it now?"

Eli's eyes heat, turning dark. "Are you sure? Like really sure? I can stop, just say the word. I won't want to, but I will."

In answer, I grab his hair and pull him down to me, sealing our lips together. Eli reaches out and cups my face in his large hands. I can feel the callouses on them. The difference of his rough skin on the smoothness of mine is amazing. I wrap a leg over his, bringing the heated space between my legs against the hardness jutting up from between his. I rotate my hips, bringing a moan from the both of us.

"Let me grab a condom. I don't want to have to stop to get one later." As he goes to move, I grab his arm.

"I have an implant. If you're clean, I'm alright with not using one."

"Why would you have a birth control implant if you're not having sex?" He's paused now, curious.

"It's part of my modeling contract. They don't want models under contract getting accidentally pregnant and ruining their schedules. They plan them out pretty far in advance for consecutive advertising spreads."

I'm a little annoyed at having to explain my reasons, but I guess he's entitled if we're going to be having sex.

"Oh, that makes sense. I'm clean. I haven't been with anyone since before training started this summer, and I always use protection. The whole team gets tested at the beginning of training every year along with any vaccinations needed and drug tests." Eli sits up, looking down at me.

"Sorry if I've killed the mood; this is a little awkward for me." He reaches out and trails his fingertips down my cheek to my throat. I tip my head back as he continues down my chest to my breasts. He swirls his fingers over one hard tip, causing an ache to bloom as he leans to kiss me. I part my lips, and he takes full advantage, slipping his tongue into my mouth to duel with mine. He switches to my other breast as he tugs my lower lip between his teeth. His touch becoming firmer, he rolls my nipple and pinches down, pulling my tongue into his mouth and sucking on it. He's over me again, and I feel his hardness twitch against my hip as I arch up and moan. God, he's going to make me come before we get far at all. I'm so worked up from the starting and stopping and now this. "I want you in me. Now."

He pulls back to look at me as he slides his hand down my side and over the little strip of hair on my pussy, gliding the back of one finger down the slit of my folds. His finger sinks in easily since I'm so wet. He gets another surprised look at the amount of slick moisture and pulls his finger back up, directly under the hood to my clit, and starts rubbing gentle circles. He's being too careful, and I want more. I trail my hands over his broad, defined shoulders and down his bicep until I get to his wrist. I put pressure on it as I raise my hips. From the look on his face, I think he gets a clue of what I want.

He twists his hand so his thumb is on my nub and sinks a finger in me all the way to the knuckle on his palm. He pumps a few times, making me hotter, then adds a second one. I gasp as he scissors his fingers, stretching me. As he presses a third in, I clutch his arms and tense up. It's getting a little too snug in there.

He pauses partway in and explains, "I need to make sure you're stretched and able to accommodate me. I'm a little larger than average, and I don't want to hurt you." He continues to push his third finger into me, and his fingers aren't small.

Eli is a big boy.

I reach out to touch him, dragging my hands down all the ridges on his abs until I get to his hard length. The tip is wet and leaking, he's so turned on. As I curl my fingers around him, he presses into my hand more fully with a groan, and I realize my fingers won't meet around him. He's also long, much longer than I expected. *Holy shit, how am I going to get that to fit?* Suddenly, I'm glad he's not going to have to breach anything, but he's bigger than others I've touched or seen in person and that's saying something as they weren't small in any capacity. I look down to see what I'm holding, and my eyes widen.

Yep, that's gonna take some maneuvering. I look back up to Eli and see a smug look on his face. Of course, he's proud of it. What guy wouldn't be? Right then, Eli starts a side to side flicking motion with his fingers curled up into that sensitive pad of flesh inside me, causing my walls to flutter around him. If he keeps that up, I'll be coming in minutes. As my breathing gets rapid and shallow and my muscles tense up, I keep eye contact.

"Let go, Remi, I want to watch you fall apart." With those words he adds a fourth finger, and this one burns as it stretches me, but I'm so wet my tightness doesn't slow him down. I twist my hips, not sure if I want to escape him or bury his hand further. My choice is made for me as he begins that scissoring motion again. I haven't taken my hands off his shoulders, and my nails are digging into his skin, but he doesn't seem to mind. He switches back to hooking his fingers up and into me, but it feels different this time. I realize he's kept two straight and pushing outwards as his middle fingers flick against that sensitive pad. I begin moving my hips in rhythm with his motions as guttural sounds begin escaping my mouth. My eyes drift to half-mast, and I give myself over to the sensations he's causing. My walls flutter harder and more rapidly, beginning to pin his fingers down.

The orgasm hits with a rush, and I clamp down on his fingers. I hear a stunned "Holy shit," from Eli as I spasm around his hand and he presses his dick firmly into my thigh, seeking relief. As I come back down, Eli slowly moves his fingers, causing little aftershocks that calm me at the same time. My thighs and asscrack are wet from my own cum. I'm a little embarrassed now that I'm done.

Eli catches my gaze again.

"Don't be shy; that was beautiful." He brings his fingers to his mouth and sucks on them. "And you taste even better than you look."

Well crap, Eli's kinda dirty, and I think I like it. *Not such a good boy, now is he?*

Not to be indelicate by bringing it up, because lord knows I really don't want to talk about other men touching you, but my fingers aren't that short, and I didn't feel any….barriers I guess would be the best word. I was hoping since I'm bigger than most that I could make it better for you by using my hand."

I'm confused for a second, distracted by the afterglow, before I get what he's talking about.

"Oh yeah, that. So, I meant what I said when I said I haven't had sex. It's just that, sex. Intercourse, with a guy. We'll just say someone else had a bit of the same idea and you won't hurt me other than what I'm going to be feeling tomorrow from what you're packing. Saddle sore is what Alex calls it."

Eli chuckles a bit at the lame joke I tacked on at the end. Details of why I don't have a hymen aren't needed right now. A major mood killer, the talk has already been serious enough.

"Okay, so I get to dive in so to speak?" Eli asks this with an expectant expression.

"Yes, can we quit talking now? I want you in me something fierce."

That takes all the amusement off his face, and the hungry look comes back. He rolls over me between my thighs, and I plant one foot on the bed and wrap the other around his hip. Eli takes the thigh of my planted leg and lifts up and out with his thick arm supporting the back of my knee.

"It'll be easier this way." As his tip reaches my entrance, he pauses. "I've never done this without a condom. If I don't last, I'll make it up to you."

With that warning he begins to push his way inside, or so I thought. His blunt tip hits my folds and slides through, but then he hits the ring of my entrance. As he presses forward, he rotates his hips a little back and forth in a small twisting motion that helps the head of his dick to begin to penetrate me. The burning intensifies, but it's not terrible, just a little uncomfortable.

Again, I'm so wet there aren't any hang-ups, just pressure.

"Normally, I would use lube, but you're so wet already that I don't think I need it. If you want some, let me know. I promise it'll feel good after you adjust." He's so sweet, if a little untimely. He can totally shut up now and just do this.

"I'm good."

I wiggle around some, and he slips in further with a grunt. His eyes are looking strained, and his mouth is open, panting a little. I can tell he just wants to push through, but he's trying to be careful. Must suck sometimes to be so well endowed. Poor guy. Or poor me, maybe. He lets the pressure off but doesn't back up. Reaching down, he rubs my clit, making me clench around him. My muscles grab onto his tip and actually seem to pull him in some with the motion. As he's pulled into me Eli starts pushing again, never letting up on my clit. I open my mouth, but no sound comes out, and he's sliding in steadily, filling me up. I feel full, and I know there's only so much actual space he can take up. He stops again and starts kissing me as I adjust. When I nudge my hips up, he drops his weight and lets gravity finish linking us. He hits bottom and grabs my hip with a hard thrust to shove deeper.

I squeal with the sensation of almost pain. He holds me there, and I can feel him flexing in his excitement. I start to throb where he's pushing in, and feel almost sick to my stomach with the fullness. I don't know if I'm going to like this, but I'm not sure how to say it without hurting his feelings. At that point he pulls halfway out, then pushes back in and hits the end again.

Alright, I'm about done, fuck that hurt. It's really not looking good for continuing. I finally get to this point and literally can't fit the guy. Only with my luck.

He looks down at me and seems crushed by the pain he must see on my face.

"Shit, baby, I'm sorry. Just hold on a sec, okay?" I nod my acquiescence.

He has about thirty seconds before I kick him off me. He pulls out almost all the way and I breathe a breath of relief. His eyes are looking very determined. He starts slow shallow thrusts with both our pelvises tipped up. In this position, he's pulling at the back of my opening and rubbing that sensitive spot right inside my pussy in a really nice way. I quickly forget that I was in pain a few seconds ago. This is awesome. I look up in shock at Eli. He has a cocky grin on his face. It says, 'I told you so.'

He picks up his pace until I'm getting worked up into another orgasm. Right before I get close enough he plunges back in, hitting the end of me and beyond, it seems, then instantly backing up to that rocking pace again before I can even register that it didn't hurt so much that time. He alternates that way for several minutes; every time I get relaxed, he quickly enters fully until I can't take it anymore. I'm thrashing my head, my hair sticking to my sweaty face, begging for him to finish it.

He doesn't comply, but now the full strokes are more complete and at the end he holds me to him tightly while flexing. I feel it building in my stomach, shooting streaks of heat through my abdomen. This feels different than getting off from his hand. I lock gazes with him as he picks up the pace, keeping a close study on my expression for his cues. He's now actually pounding me hard, and I'm loving it, arching my back up with my head back, barely able to keep my eyes open. I feel my impending release and tighten like a fist around his girth as it begins. It comes hard and deep, and before the first wave crashes over I hear Eli mutter 'shit' as he closes his eyes and groans. My tightening walls have locked him in, and all he can do is flex his hips and rub them in circles as he loses control and starts to come. He's desperately trying to rub my clit in a rhythm to bring me with him, but the pulsing of his shaft buried so deep with the rocking he's doing is bringing it on hard. It swells over me, making my stomach muscles clench tight as I wrap myself around him and trap his hand between my legs and his head in my arms as I hang on until the spasms loosen.

Again, Holy Shit.

Seems about all I can say tonight. *That's just not normal,* I think as we both begin to relax and I catch my breath. I'm going to have a charlie horse after that. Eli looks down at me with a wondrous smile, still holding me tight.

"I love you, Remi." I freeze. *Can I do it? Sure as shit can, girlfriend. Buck up and tell him.*

"I love you too, Eli," I whisper, almost afraid to hear it aloud, as if he'll reject it, even if he did tell me first. His smile is brilliant. He swoops in for a kiss, and we don't come up for air for several minutes. By now he's gone mostly flaccid and slipped out of me along with a bit of a mess.

He gives me a few pecks on the lips. "Hold on," he says as he gets up. "Let me get cleaned up." He walks into his bathroom, and I hear water running. After a minute, he comes back with a washcloth. I reach to take it, but he shakes his head. "I made the mess, and I'll clean it up." I blush bright red as he looks down directly at me, splayed legs and all, even though we just made love.

He leans over and kisses near my belly button then takes the warm cloth to gently clean me. When he pulls back, it's slightly tinted pink.

"I'm sorry, baby. I don't think you're bleeding, maybe just bumped your cervix a little much." I look at him curiously. Why would a guy know so much about the female anatomy? He must have seen the question on my face. "Not to sound conceited, but I've always had a hard time, being so big. I took a couple women's studies classes. I wasn't pushing into you to hurt you. I was trying to see if I could get you to stretch and get you tented." Tented, what the fuck is he talking about this for? "Tenting, it's why I got you off first, you know, so you could accommodate better?"

"Oh my god, Eli, I know what tenting is. Thank you for all the consideration. I really appreciated it. Please, can we stop talking about my vagina tenting?!"

I'm freaking mortified. I hop up and go to the toilet, leaving the door partially ajar. I mean, really, we did just have sex. A little tinkle noise shouldn't offend Dr. Vagina out there.

"You know, it's good to know your body. We're both adults and should be able to discuss our mutual sexual heath." He sounds a little put out.

"I'm embarrassed, Eli. I went over the important parts beforehand, maybe give it a few times before the more in depth discussion, m'kay? Most guys, hell, even most girls I know, don't just sit around and discuss this. I'm glad you're good with it. Just, let's discuss it a little less for now? It was awesome. I trusted you. I was a little nervous, I'll admit, but it got good quickly. Now that you've cleaned us both up can we please cuddle like normal people?" Eli tosses the rag into the empty clothes basket and hops in under the blanket with me.

"Say it again." It's not a request; it's a demand.

"I love you, Eli."

I snuggle into him with my head on his chest and our arms around each other. He kisses the top of my head, resting his chin there. I could stay here forever. I want to stay awake longer and bask in this, but I'm so sleepy. It's been a long night. He whispers against me, "I love you, Remi." That's the last thing I hear as I drift off after the best orgasms ever.

❦ ❦ ❦

A door slams, waking me up. I instantly tense, worried about someone getting in here. I shake Eli awake.

"Do you hear that? Someone's in here." I can hear the panic in my voice, and Eli is alert in seconds.

"Stay here. I'll go look." I hear more moving around in the living room. More than one person. Someone in the main hall, then I hear the apartment door open. I quickly wrap the sheet around me. Eli has pulled on a pair of boxers.

"Hola, bitches!" This comes in an English accent. Odd sounding doesn't begin to cover it. Eli visibly relaxes.

"Brother, will you shut the bloody hell up? I'm too tired for your shit." Another of the same voice and accent.

"Will you two idiots move? I'd like to put my stuff down eventually. It is almost five. *In the morning.* I would like to get to bed."

Yet another voice. Also with an accent, but a different one. Australian, if my ears don't deceive me. I stiffen in Eli's embrace. I cannot believe I'm hearing that voice. Not now. Eli groans and gets up, going out the bedroom door.

I jump up and walk out of Eli's bedroom, not even caring that I'm in only a sheet. I know I must be as pale as it as well. I'm standing behind Eli and can't quite see more than three human-shaped shadows in the dark room.

"What the fuck, Eli. You have a girl over the minute we're gone? You know the hook ups don't come here. We've discussed this, and you're not one to bring them here anyway. You go to their place or the back of a car or wherever. Not here." He turns to speak to me, peering around Eli. "I don't know who you are, but it's time to leave. I'm not in the mood, so hurry up. Eli, get your booty call out of here."

Eli is about to blow.

Hell, I'm about to blow. That stick up his ass hasn't moved a bit. I'd know that voice and attitude anywhere. It didn't usually used to be directed at me though. I think I'm in shock, both with who is here and what he said.

"Don't talk to her like-" Eli stops when I say one word.

"Ethan?" I inquire softly, but all three turn to look at me. I see them trying to make out who I am in the dark room behind Eli. Then I realize I know the others as well. "Oh my god, Beckett? Dylan? What the hell are you doing here?" My voice is as outraged as my thoughts. Variations of puzzlement flash across their faces. Ethan's clears first.

"Reese cup? Oh, fuck me." With that, he darts across the room, dropping everything he had in his hands. Grabbing me and roughly pulling me to him, he crushes his mouth down on mine. I don't even think to protest because I'm so shocked. This isn't possible. How did this happen? My thoughts are tumbling through my head without any logical answers. Before I can do anything at all, I hear Eli.

"What the hell, Ethan? Get off my girlfriend." Eli grabs me and forcibly pulls me behind him.

"Your girlfriend?" Ethan looks stricken.

I'm just staring, my gaze going from one to the two others. It's apparent when they recognize me.

"Remi?"

"Duckie?" They both start forward.

Mirror images of each other. They've grown quite a bit since I last saw them when they were sixteen, but it's still their beautiful faces. Black as a ravens hair, crystal blue eyes, sharp angular features. Taller than both the others in the room. I see they've quite grown into the gangly forms they used to have. Trim and ripped, not as bulked up as Eli, but streamlined.

They're both so beautiful.

Not that they weren't years ago, but maturity has put the icing on these cupcakes. I see that Beck has three studs in his left ear and a small hoop in his lip. Other than clothing, that's the only difference I see. As they reach the two guys in front of me, I come around to them. They sweep me up a in hug simultaneously. I'm so shocked and happy too that I don't know if I should laugh or cry. When I say as much, they just hold me tighter. It's been so long since I was wrapped between these two like this. I finally pull away when I hear Eli and Ethan arguing. It's then that I realize what a mess this is about to be. Both twins drop kisses on my lips as I back up. Neither Eli nor Ethan miss the move.

Shit's about to get interesting.

"Remi, how do you know the guys? Is that why you kept asking about who lived here?" This from Eli, who's now sounding suspicious and not just a little hurt.

"I didn't know they lived here or even that there was a possibility. I really was just curious about the owners. I do know Ethan from a few years ago though. Right before my dad...well, you know. Things didn't really end well, did they, Ethan?" I say coldly as I turn to him. Now I'm getting mad, remembering exactly why we broke up. "You took off after your dad made me go home and never spoke to me again. I called you, and your dad told me you were busy. When I came by the next day when you didn't answer your cell, I was told by the housekeeper that you and your parents had left that morning and that she was to close up the house indefinitely." I'm almost yelling at the end. All the anger and hurt has come back. I calm myself and turn to the twins.

"Now these two I can't be mad at. Their dad sent them off to military school after getting into trouble with me. Back then I thought it was in England.." I'm beginning to put all this together now. I don't know why it wasn't obvious before. The motorcycle, the familiar scents. The meeting at school before being roommates, the coin I found in Eli's room that I was going to ask him about… "You all went to the same military school, didn't you?" I look directly at Eli. There's no way he didn't know. Is this all a sick game? "Ethan, I thought you went back to Australia, but you were in the U.S. the whole time, weren't you? And Beck? Dylan? You were here too? You never tried to call or write or send up a smoke signal?" I'm so mad that I feel angry tears coming on. Everything was so great a few minutes ago. Now my life has come crashing down again as par for the course. I need to get out of here; I refuse to cry in front of them all. "I think I'm going to take a shower now. Eli? I'll see you in the morning. Or later in the morning, I guess. Guys, it was nice to see you. I'll be out of your hair as soon as possible." My words are stiff and my spine more so as I turn and hurry to my room. Eli starts to come after me, calling my name. I hold up my hand to stop him. He can get his sheet later; I doubt he's hopping back into bed right now anyway.

As I go to my room and close the door, the conversation starts back up. It's apparent they're talking about me. I can't believe the way Ethan spoke to me, even if he didn't know it was me. They're practically strangers now, and I shouldn't have let any of them touch me. Unsure about how this is going to turn out with Eli, I know I can't be over here while they are. I throw my dirty clothes in the hamper and adjust the water. As it heats up, the first of the tears start. I feel like I'm losing them all at once all over again, and now Eli's added in with that.

I stay in there for a long time before finally getting out and dressed in lounge clothes. With my fuzzy socks on and hair pulled up, I start packing.

I have my two suitcases and the two plastic totes in the closet, so thankfully there's no need to go out and see anyone. I know I told Eli I would see him later, but right now, it's going to be *much* later. After putting my laptop and school work in my backpack along with my purse, I pack all my clothes into the suitcases and gather my toiletries out of the bathroom so it can be cleaned.

I'm paused by the door after stripping the bed and cleaning the bathroom, surveying the room for anything else that needs attention, when I hear a knock on the door.

"Remi?" It's Eli. "Can I come in?"

I keep my voice steady, I've had enough with the crying.

"I don't think so, Eli. Can you just please go? I'll see you later, alright? I just want to be alone right now, please. I don't want to talk about any of." I hear him move away from the door.

It hurts.

I know I won't see him like this again. I can't. Not as long as he's here. As long as *they're* here. My plans with Alex seem impossible again. Just like when my life got postponed after my dad. I don't want to think about seeing any of the three in public. I'm frantic and numb at the same time. I think maybe I'm in a bit of shock.

It's official. I have the worst luck ever.

I go over the room one last time to be sure that I didn't leave anything behind. The only other places I need to check would be the living room or kitchen.

After I hear it get quiet and several doors close, I make my way out with the dirty bedding, to the laundry room and put it in to wash. I decide to leave the soap I bought. I can get more. The less to carry out of here, the better. I want to be gone before anyone comes out of their rooms.

Checking the dryer I see I have clothes in there, and take them out to quietly head back to my room. I dump them in the open suitcase and go back out, trying not to make noise. Grabbing the few things I see of mine, I take them into my room to put them in the totes.

I decide not to worry about the clothes I took off in Eli's room, no way am I going to go in there to get them. I can't talk to him right now. I get the suitcases down to my car just as it's getting light outside. I go back for a tote; I'll have to make another trip for the last one. I write a quick note to Eli that I'm sorry, but I can't stay here and that I left the bedding in the wash. I slide the note under his door on my way to get the last tote.

There's a package wrapped in bright purple paper on my bed. The tag says Love, Eli. He must not have been sleeping, and I appreciate him giving me my space for now. I put the package in my backpack so I can open it later. He knows I'm leaving, and being the sweetheart that he is, he's not going to try to stop me. I don't doubt for a minute that he won't track me down soon, or maybe not, depending on what the guys told him. I don't know how this mess happened. There is no way this is complete coincidence.

As I get in my car, I turn to look up at the brownstone. I'm not sure how, but I'm going to have to avoid them as much as possible. I just need a few days to get over the surprise of it. I've gone without seeing them for years, so it shouldn't even matter anymore. I feel my bare neck. I haven't taken that locket off except to swim or shower since the twins gave it to me. I left it laying open on the nightstand in the room I stayed in.

On one side a picture of the twins and on the other a picture of Ethan…

Epilogue

Elliot

She's gone. I know it as soon as I get to her door. It's slightly ajar, and I can see the bed has been stripped and the desk is bare. I don't go further in; I don't need to. I walk into the living area and see the note on the island. It's about fucking laundry and that she needs to not be here.

That's it.

No mention of anything else. I don't understand. I mean, I get that something is up with the other guys, and that's just surreal, but she could have stayed with me. I hear a noise behind me.

"She left?" I turn to see it's Ethan. His hair is standing on end, probably a lot like mine and probably from the same reason of running his hands through it in irritation.

"Are you surprised? Should I be? Maybe you could tell me. You and the others seem to know her better than I do."

I'm bitter, and I think I have every right to be. I knew there was a girl in all their pasts. I just didn't know it was the same one and that it was going to totally screw me over. I run my hands through my hair again.

"Well, this is a fine situation we're finding ourselves in. Can't ever say I expected to finally hook back up with Reese by finding her in my friend's bed. I think we all owe each other an explanation. Let's wait on the twins to get up. And to answer your question, no, I'm not too surprised she took off, but you'll understand better once we tell you our stories. Not sure how I didn't piece together what I know of the twin's story with mine either. Some professional I am." Ethan links his fingers behind his neck and blows out a breath. I haven't even asked how the assignment went. It can wait for now.

I hear an exclamation from Remi's room.

"Beck! She's gone!" Dylan sounds upset. Usually he's the quieter and more steady of the two, so I'm surprised at the volume and panic in his tone. Beck is the one prone to dramatics.

I follow Ethan to Remi's room to find Beckett and Dylan standing next to the night stand. "Beckett, she still had it." He looks up at his brother with sad eyes. "Was she wearing this before?" The question is directed at me.

"Yeah, I never saw her without it. I asked her once about it, and she said she'd tell me sometime. Really hadn't gotten around to it, I guess. What's in it? I've never seen it open." I peer over and see the twins and Ethan. Ethan must be looking as well as I hear him inhale sharply.

"She didn't forget us, brother. We shouldn't have left her alone for so long." Barely a whisper to begin with, Beck's voice cracks on the end of the sentence.

"Hey, Dylan? Hand me that book, please?"

I notice the Alice book that used to sit on the desk as Ethan asks for it in the partially open nightstand drawer. When he gets it, he opens it to the cover and runs his finger across something written there. Over his shoulder I see it's an inscription addressed to Reece to always remember reading the stories together and taking the leap down the rabbit hole with him. It's signed E-

"You're the friend that gave her the book. I was worried she had been in your room when I first saw it. Explains a lot about yours though." I think maybe I should have kept my mouth shut as Ethan throws me a look, but I can't seem to stop it. "You're also one of the one's she told me about." I think about my next words carefully; these are my friends here. "Straight up, I'll do whatever I can to get her back. She only left because you all showed up. You're my best friends, but I love her, and I'm not sharing."

They all look at me, but no one comments on the sharing thing, like I didn't even mention it.

"We'll get her back. We need to have a discussion, and we also need to share our stories. Eli, how did you end up with her?" Ethan looks at me. I sit down on the corner of her bed.

"Remember the girl I told you I was seeing before you left? That was Remi." I'm not sure how I'm going to deal with whatever the guys want from her, but I know I refuse to give her up. I finally just found my one person to be with, and I love her. She is mine. A thought occurs to me, confusing me further. "How did you not know she was around? Her best friend has been a student here for two years, and I've never heard you mention her before..."

"We never met a friend and didn't bother to look for one here. I guess we should start at the beginning. Beck, Dylan? You guys met her first, I'm guessing? You want to start?" Beck takes the locket and closes it. Dragging the chain through his fingers, he starts.

"Remi was fifteen, we were sixteen...."

Adam

I ring the buzzer downstairs to see Remi. She and Eli took off from the party last night, and we didn't get to hang out like I had hoped. I'm not sure if I have a chance with Eli in the picture. She seems really into him. The door opens, and instead of me going up, a man is standing there.

"Can I help you?" He has an Australian accent and doesn't look very happy to see me.

"Is Remi home?" I'm hoping this is a roommate and not a new friend.

"She's not here."

I frown. I was sure she had planned to stay in today.

"Do you know where she went?" I had already tried to call her and hadn't gotten an answer.

"No, I have to go. When I see her, I'll let her know you stopped by." He closes the door without even asking my name. Something's off. I'll send her a text and then get ahold of her friend Alex later if she doesn't answer.

I pull out my phone to report in.

Remington

I let myself into Alex's apartment. I didn't see her roommate's car outside, so I'm hoping she's not here and that Alex is home.

Alone preferably.

I make my way toward her room and drop my bags in the spare one on the way, deciding to get the rest of my stuff out of the car later. Knocking twice when I get to her door, I peek in when she doesn't answer. I hear the shower running in the en suite.

"Alex?" I yell.

"Remi? In here."

At least I think she's alone. I don't think she'd invite me in if she had company. I go in the bathroom and hop up onto the counter.

"What's up? I figured you'd be a little busy today with Eli?"

"So did I. Some people showed up last night."

Alex pokes her head out, hair dripping on the floor. "People?"

"Yeah, umm, do you remember me telling you about Ethan?" Alex nods her head yes. "And Dylan and Beck?"

"Yes, but what do they have to do with you not being with Eli?" She looks confused

"Well, they're all Eli's roommates. That live in the same building. Together." I'm waiting, and it doesn't take very long for the lightbulb to go off.

"Oh, shit. Did you and Eli?" I nod. I must look pretty miserable because she pops back in the shower without saying anything, and a minute later is out, wrapped in a towel and then engulfing me in a hug.

"I don't know what to do, Alex. I packed everything when they all went to bed and came here."

"You can stay here. I'd imagine it would be uncomfortable with them all there. I'll talk to my roommate and let her know you'll be here a while. Don't worry about how long. I'll deal with it." I love Alex; she's always there for me, as I am for her. "You tell me all about everything, and it'll help you decide what to do with Eli."

"Before we get to that, there are a few things I never told you about the others. I was kind of embarrassed and confused. I didn't mean to hide anything, it's just…I don't know. Still confused, I guess." Alex gets dressed, looking a little hurt that I'd keep secrets but mostly curious. I start my story, this time leaving nothing out.

"It was the first year you were gone to your grandparents in Florida the whole summer. I was fifteen, and they were sixteen…"

About the Author

Emma Cole is an indie author that writes across the genre board. Nothing is off limits, so that means mature audiences only. From light and fluffy to down and dirty—if it strikes her fancy and has a story to tell she's on it.

Want to stalk the author? You can catch her on most platforms!

Facebook

Page- Emma Cole

Readers Group- Emma's Author Stalkers

Other Works by Emma Cole

Remington Carter Series

Echoes

Requiem

Clarity

(coming July 2020)

The Dark Duet

Lark

Nightingale

Death Dealers- Serial

Episode One

Episode Two
Episode Three
(coming soon)

Wicked Reform School Series
Avarice: House of Mustelid

Purr-fect Portrait: A Pet Play Short Story

The Order: Hit and Run- A Dark Paranormal Bully Romance

Made in the USA
Monee, IL
15 October 2022

15948748R00118